OBSESSION AND DECEPTION

First Edition

Published by The Nazca Plains Corporation
Las Vegas, Nevada
2010

ISBN: 978-1-935509-99-8

Published by

The Nazca Plains Corporation ®
4640 Paradise Rd, Suite 141
Las Vegas NV 89109-8000

PUBLISHER'S NOTE
Obsession and Deception is a work of fiction created wholly by *Hank Brooks'* imagination. All characters are fictional and any resemblance to any persons living or deceased is purely by accident. No portion of this book reflects any real person or events.

Cover, Blake Stephens
Art Director, Blake Stephens

DEDICATION

This book is dedicated to all my gay friends who helped me through a rough transition when I came out, and who became my second family.

OBSESSION AND DECEPTION

First Edition

Hank Brooks

- CHAPTER ONE -

I woke up from some deep sleep. I felt like I was stepping out of an abyss. My head was throbbing. How did I get such an awful headache? I couldn't figure out where I was. Something bad had happened, but I couldn't remember what. When I tried to open my eyes everything was a blur. All I could figure out was that I was in a bed, and as I glanced around I could see that I had an IV in my arm. If I had been able to see further down I would have seen the catheter in my prick. I guessed I was in a hospital, and no matter how hard I tried I could not remember coming here.

I tried to look around and figure out where I was, and if indeed it was a hospital. With great effort I turned my neck. There was a bed next to mine and I could see a body in it. I couldn't even tell what sex it was. Its head was all bandaged and one arm and one leg were in casts. This prompted me to look down, and I could tell that I had no casts on me. The body in the bed had an IV stuck in its arm also, and I clearly saw a catheter bag hanging from the side of its bed. At some point, I heard a moan. The sound was a deep baritone and I decided that my room mate was a guy.

I forced myself to concentrate. Try to remember. Try to remember. The harder I tried the more I desired sleep and as usual my desires were greater than my intellect. I fell into a deep sleep. I had no idea that I was receiving heavy doses of various pain killers. I didn't know it at that time either, but I slept for nearly thirty-six hours more.

When I awoke my head and my vision were somewhat clearer. I looked over at my room mate. His bandaged head was turned toward me, and I heard him ask with great difficulty, "Are you awake?"

"Yes, at least I think so. How long have I been here?"

"I think we've been here about four days," he answered.

I hesitated before admitting to him that I had no memory of how I got here.

"They brought us in together in the same ambulance. There was an accident, a terrible accident," he informed me. I racked my brain. I tried so hard to remember, and I fell asleep again.

The next time I woke up I hoped that my healing had finally begun. My head was much clearer and hardly ached at all. I could clearly see that I was indeed in a hospital, but I still did not remember how I got here. I glanced over to my room mate. He was smiling at me and he had no bandage on his head, but he still had the casts.

"Welcome back," he said.

"Hi," I responded. What happened?"

"Don't you remember?" he asked, and then answered his own question. "We were in a bus accident, a real lulu. Seven people were killed, mostly elementary school kids, and two from our bus." He choked with emotion and couldn't say any more.

"Did you know any of them?" I asked.

He turned his head from me, letting me know that he didn't want to or couldn't talk about it. "No," he stated in a whisper and I sensed that our conversation was ended for now.

I forced my brain to try to remember, and for a second I got a flash. I remembered boarding a bus, then a gap in memory. I remembered the sound of impact, and flailing bodies being tossed all over the bus. I remembered seeing the nose of another bus coming into our space and I knew that whoever sat in the seats where impact occurred could not possibly have survived.

But what was I doing on the bus? Where was I going? I could not remember. The strain of trying sent me right back to sleep for I do not know how many more hours.

When I awoke the next time, the room was dark and I could tell it was night time. There was a TV in the room and it was turned on, but no sound came from it. I glanced over at my room mate. His bed was cranked up so that he was almost in a sitting position. His eyes were closed and I suspected that he had fallen asleep watching television. He was snoring lightly so I said nothing to him, and I was pleased to see that his catheter bag was gone, but not the IV.

I watched the silent TV for some time and then a nurse came in and turned it off. Somehow I managed to fall asleep again. This sleep was different from the other drug induced sleeps. I had fallen asleep naturally and I had a dream. When I awoke I remembered the dream and I remembered at last how I came to be in a hospital in Ft. Lauderdale, Florida. I was able to remember back to a time about six months earlier, when I left home, and to a time shortly before that.

I was an eighteen year old Mormon boy living in Boise, Idaho. I obeyed all the rules of the church and studied my Bible meticulously. When I went to bed at night my prayers were not just prayers and recitals from the liturgy, they were supplications to God. I prayed that he would not send me to hell for being gay. I had never acted on my sexual orientation, but I believed that God knew everything, and so He most certainly must know about me. I fell asleep every night, praying for salvation.

Try as I might, and pray as I might, I could not deny my nature. I searched the net, and entered forbidden chat rooms until I met a seventeen year old who told me that he was a Mormon also, and that he was suffering the same guilt that I was experiencing. We made dates to message each other on line when we were both available. Finally we agreed to meet in a park which my IM buddy heard was a well known cruising area.

I was scared to death, but I proceeded to our rendez-vous at the appointed hour. I was to wear a white tee shirt with blue denim shorts and he was to wear a blue tee shirt with white denim shorts. We had described our physical appearances to each other and sent pictures in E Mails so I was certain I would not miss the guy I knew only as Hung123. It bothered me that we had not given each other our real names.

I walked along a path he had described to me, and out of the darkness I heard someone call my screen name. "Hotboy?"

I looked around and saw nothing, but then a body emerged from the darkness. He looked nothing like the pictures in the E Mails. This was a man of at least forty, big burly and ugly. I had been entrapped by a vice cop. Since I was of legal age and had arranged to meet a minor for purposes of sex, I was truly busted.

He pulled my arms behind my back and handcuffed me. He read me my rights and before I knew what had happened to me I was in the police station and they called my parents.

My father knew several of the police officers from our church. Because he was a Church Elder, and to avoid shame befalling our church, they let me go. I was released into his custody with stern warnings.

In the car going home my parents were silent, but as soon as we entered the house, my father said, "You can take one small suitcase and pack a few necessities. I will see to it that you are excommunicated from the Church for homosexuality. I want you out of my house in half an hour and I never want to see you again." My mother was sitting in a chair with her face to the wall. She could not bear to look at me.

As I left the house, my mother followed me out to the front porch. She never spoke to me, but she stuffed something into my pocket. When I looked a little while later it was ninety-five dollars in small bills. I also had managed to take about sixty dollars of my own money which I had saved from some small part time jobs. In total, I left home with $155.00. I thought of using the money for a bus ticket out of Boise, but I decided to save as much as I could. Instead I hitchhiked to San Francisco. By the time I got there, I still had $150.00.

I found a small furnished room. I needed to give the landlord fifty dollars as a security deposit and fifty for the first month's rent. I put my meager belongings in my room and immediately went searching for a job. I was a high school graduate and was due to start BYU in the fall, but now that would never be. I had no trouble getting a job in a Wendy's just two streets from where I now lived.

It was easy locating gay bars in San Francisco, but I was too shy to go in. I would walk by them non-chalantly and try to look inside, but my feet would not allow entrance. I did find one place that had a little magazine stand outside the front entrance. There was always a supply of free gay periodicals in the racks. At least I was able to work up the courage to walk up to the rack one day and arm myself with the magazines.

The magazines were fully loaded with ads for gay bars, massages, escorts, and an assortment of gay owned businesses, none of which interested me. One ad, however, caught my full attention. It was for a travel agency that specialized in gay cruises. They gave an 800 number to call for information, brochures etc. I became convinced that a cruise was my best chance to meet other gay men in a safe environment. I would be seated at a dinner table with three, five or seven other guys. I could meet them in a friendly setting. I screwed up my courage and called the agency. To my delight everything was automated. I didn't have to speak to anyone living. I requested brochures of the upcoming trips for the next six months.

Most of the trips were Caribbean cruises and left from Miami or Ft. Lauderdale's Port Everglades. They ranged from five days to 10 days. The single cabins were much more expensive than the doubles, but the best part of it was that if you did not have anyone to share a cabin with, they would match you with someone in similar circumstances. The worst part was that in addition to the posted price, you would have to fly to Florida at your own expense.

I zeroed in on an eight day trip which stopped at several ports. It was four months away, falling between Thanksgiving and Christmas when the rates were at their lowest. If I didn't take any expensive side trips, the cost with tips, tax and airfare would be approximately $2,250.00. In the few short weeks I had lived in San Francisco, I had managed to save $500.00. I ate at least two meals a day at the restaurant, and skipped the third meal. I didn't go to the bars or the movies. If I could get a credit card with a maximum credit cap of a mere $2,500.00, and if I could get the time off, I could have the whole trip paid off in no time.

I asked for and got double shifts at work, and was able to procure a VISA card with a $3000.00 credit cap. I spoke to my boss, who said it would be tough to manage without me, but he gave me the time off. I immediately called the 800 number and was able to secure a double cabin with another single man. They told me he was fifty two years old and lived in New York. I readily agreed to share the cabin with him. Since I had no computer, they mailed me a bunch of papers to complete and return.

I spent hours filling out the papers. I didn't want to fuck up anything and destroy my opportunity to take the cruise. I also had some hard decisions to make. In the end, I decided to take trip cancellation insurance. It wasn't cheap, but if I had to cancel for some unknown reason, it would be cheap at that.

The next decision was a no brainer. The papers explained that Port Everglades was very close to the airport, and a cab ride would probably be less than $15.00. However, the cruise line was providing a bus from the airport to the ship at no cost. It would be leaving at 11:30 AM from Terminal 2 on the day of the cruise. The same offer was good for the return trip, and the bus would leave the pier at noon on the day we arrived back in Florida.

I checked the airlines and the least expensive air fare was a red eye which would get me to Ft. Lauderdale at 5:45 AM. I could return on a 6 PM flight which would get me to San Francisco about 8 PM due to the time difference. After I was safely booked on my flights, I accepted the offer of the bus service. I read the completed papers over carefully several times, and booked the entire trip on my credit card. I took my packet to the post office and sent it out certified, return receipt requested. It was bad enough that I was alone in the world, the last thing I needed was another fuck up in my life.

All that was left for me was to work hard and make as much money as possible. I didn't mind the double shifts at all. This was to be the trip of my lifetime. By the time I was a week away from departure, I had saved another $750.00. I would have saved more, but I bought some clothes for the trip. The cruise line had sent a list of recommended attire, and I filled in what I needed. I also made two payments on my credit card which were billed to me after the initial charges and before the trip itself. My debt was minimal and I was feeling pretty good about life in general. I even thought of going to one of the bars, but I always chickened out.

Instead I would lie in bed at night and fantasize that I would meet a handsome young man on the ship. Of course he would fall instantly in love with me. I whacked off every night, as my phantom lover sucked my cock and fucked me until I could barely tolerate the ecstasy.

I posted a huge calendar in the entrance hall of my studio apartment and at the end of every day I crossed out the day just ended. Time seemed to crawl and then miraculously it was time for me to go to the airport to catch my red-eye. My manager volunteered to drive me there and I gladly accepted his offer. When we arrived at the terminal he opened his trunk, and I removed my suitcase. I extended my hand to shake his, and to thank him for the ride and for volunteering to pick me up as well. Imagine my amazement when he took my hand, pulled me to him, and kissed me full on the lips.

"Have a great time, Aaron," he whispered, "and come home to me safely." Before I could react in any way, he was back in his car and he took off, leaving me standing there with my mouth hanging open.

The trip to Florida was without incident. I slept most of the way, dreaming about the possibility of making love to Brad, my manager. He was only twenty-two and very good looking or at least I thought so. We arrived just before 6 AM. It was only 3 AM in San Francisco and I felt cheated out of sleep. After I retrieved my suitcase, I took a shuttle bus to Terminal 2. There I found a coffee shop and had breakfast. I lingered over breakfast as long as possible, but finally I went outside and sat on a bench waiting for the cruise bus even though it was not scheduled for hours. I sat on the bench and maybe for the hundredth time I checked to make sure I had my passport and all the travel documents that the cruise line had given me. I even affixed my room tag on my suitcase. As far as I could tell, I was all set.

Somehow the time passed, and a bus pulled up. Its sides were emblazoned with the names of several cruise lines and the words, 'Shuttle Bus' so there was no doubt that this was the bus I was looking for. As soon as the bus pulled up to the curb, the doors opened and the driver came out to light a cigarette. I asked him if this was the bus to 'Sea Nymph,' the name of my ship.

"Yes," he answered. "There are three ships leaving today. We'll be picking up passengers for all of them, and we'll be pulling out in less than an hour." Then he disappeared. The bus filled up quickly, and no other bus came along. I figured out that it was first come, first served for this freebie and if I hadn't gotten my papers in quickly, I probably would have needed a taxi right about now. I was quick to realize that not every passenger on this shuttle bus was going to be gay. Passengers were being dropped off at the three cruise lines. I was right. There were an equal number of men and women aboard.

When the bus was full, the driver reappeared. He got on the public address system, announced the names of the ships in the order he would arrive at them and urged us to be ready to depart the bus. My ship was last. I noticed that the driver seemed to slur his words and uneasiness invaded my body.

The bus pulled away from the curb and headed out of the airport. I could see a sign with an arrow pointing straight ahead. It read "I-595" and right after it another sign read, "Port Everglades 3 Miles" Wow it really was close. As the driver approached the entrance ramp to the highway, I began to get an uneasy feeling. He wasn't slowing down at all, yet all the signs clearly read, "YIELD."

He entered the highway at a speed of at least seventy miles per hour and crossed over the right lane of traffic at a forty five degree angle. It was then I heard the screech of wheels and several feet of the front end of a school bus penetrated our bus. Bodies flew everywhere. The last thing I remember thinking was, "Why was that idiot driver trying to kill us?"

Then I lost consciousness.

- Chapter Two -

I turned to my hospital room mate. He was staring at me, and I thought he was kind of cute. He was probably in his early twenties so he was older than I. He had a blanket covering most of his body, and I couldn't make out much more of him

"I'm Aaron," I said to him. "I remember everything now."

He started to answer me, but a nurse came into the room.

"Well, how are you today Mr. Jackson? You are looking bright eyed this morning. The doctor will be in to see you shortly." Then much to my embarrassment, she began to bathe me. Thank God, she handed me a damp wash cloth and I did my own privates. I was amazed at how deftly she changed the bed linen with me still in the bed. When she was finished she removed my surgical dressings, and applied an antiseptic solution around the wound and the drainage tubes. Then she put on fresh dressings.

"I'll bet the doctor removes your catheter and the drainage tubes soon and the stitches in two or three days. You won't need dressings after that," she commented. "I'm also pretty sure that the doctor will want us to get you out of bed today." She directed her attention to my room mate, and repeated the bathing routine on him, and also changed his linen.

As soon as she left, breakfast was delivered to our room. It seems I was on a liquid diet, and they served me apple juice, clear broth (for breakfast) and black coffee. All I could down was the juice.

My room mate finally spoke. "My name's Carl Gilmore," he said.

"Aaron Jackson," I echoed. "It's nice to meet you. Where are you from?"

"San Francisco."

"Me too," I told him and I was really surprised. We then compared notes and found out that we had been on the same flight coming to Florida, and had the same flight going home. We were also going on the same gay cruise, or rather, not going.

"I think we'll have to call the airline to cancel our return flight. As soon as the doctor tells us when, we can reschedule our flight home, but it doesn't look like it will be any time soon, at least not for me. I have a broken arm and a broken leg and they tell me you had your spleen and liver punctured and both were surgically repaired."

"Wow," was all I could manage to say. "I have no medical insurance," I confided in him.

"You don't have to worry about it. The driver was high on cocaine and the cruise line is footing the bill. They're also returning or crediting us the complete cost of the trip including air fare. A couple of lawyers have been in to get us to start a joint suit against them, but I told them I wanted to talk to you about it first." He paused because what he was about to say was really painful.

"A man and a woman were killed at the point of impact, and you and I were hospitalized. Several other guys were treated at the scene and released, but I feel awful for those kids on the school bus. Five of them were killed outright and fifteen more were hospitalized. They have all since been released except for one little boy, and they don't think he'll make it."

"That's the pits," I agreed.

Just then a man in a lab coat entered the room. "Hello, Dr. Berriman," Carl said. The doctor drew the curtain separating our beds, and began his daily examination of Carl's body. I could hear the conversation between them. It seems that all of Carl's bruises were healing nicely. He could be discharged in a couple of days and the cruise line was putting him up in a hotel near the hospital until the casts were removed and he was approved for flying. In the meantime they would give him crutches and a walking cast.

Then the doctor came to my bedside. He sat on a chair and extended his hand which I shook. "I'm Dr. Berriman," he said. "We know that your name is Aaron Jackson. We got that from your wallet. But we could not find any other names to call to advise them of your condition."

"What is my condition?" I asked.

"Well, you'll be just fine. Some of your vital organs were damaged, but we've repaired them and you are doing well. I'm going to remove your catheter and your drainage tubes today, and put you on a soft diet. I'll remove your stitches in a day or two, and you'll be good to go home the day after that. Now tell me. Is there anyone you want to notify?"

I should call my boss and my landlord," I answered, "but I can do that myself if you'd like."

"No," the doctor said. "It's best I call them. I wouldn't want them to think you're kidding and playing hooky." He wrote their numbers on a prescription pad, and then he removed my catheter and my drainage tubes.

When I said I had to pee, he handed me a urinal and said, "Use this for now. The nurses are going to get you out of bed for a while this afternoon." He pulled back the curtain and the first thing I saw was Carl smiling at me. He was really cute.

With morning baths and breakfast out of the way, Carl and I were undisturbed for awhile. We talked and talked and got to really know each other. I told him my story and how I got excommunicated and kicked out of the house and then he told me his story.

He was born and raised in San Francisco. His parents were religious fundamentalists, not unlike Mormons, and when he was nineteen, they caught him having sex with his father's brother who was twenty-five. His father kicked him out and his grandfather disowned his uncle. His uncle had a little money, and he told Carl he was going to Los Angeles. Carl hadn't seen or heard from him since.

Carl got a job at a Burger King. In the beginning, he slept in shelters, but eventually he rented a furnished studio apartment just as I had done, in the same neighborhood. Now five years later he managed the store and expected to be made a regional manager in the near future. He had a nice one bedroom apartment in a good neighborhood, and his future looked promising. When he was through telling his story, he looked at me squarely in the eyes, and said, "The only thing I need now is someone to share my future with."

"That's just fantastic," I said. "I'm headed in the same direction as you are, and you have given me great hope. I don't feel so lost any more. Do you think you and I might get together sometime when we get home?"

"For sure," he answered. "If you hadn't asked, I would have." He smiled his wonderful smile at me.

In the middle of the afternoon, my phone rang. I was shocked at the unexpected sound, but managed to pick up the handset. It was Brad, and he sounded hysterical. I told him to calm down and I related the whole story to him. I assured him that I would probably be home in a week or a little longer. I asked him to please call my landlord and fill him in as well. When I hung up, I saw that Carl had dozed off. It occurred to me that both Brad and Carl seemed interested in me. The thought was overwhelming. I didn't have much time to dwell on it when I dozed off also. I was awakened when the evening nurse came in to get me out of bed. Boy was I glad to see him.

He placed a chair at the side of my bed on Carl's side. He put his hands on my back and helped me sit up. Then he put my feet over the side of the bed and helped me stand. I stood still accepting his support. Then he made me take a few steps which thoroughly exhausted me, so he helped me sit down on the chair between the beds.

"I'll be back in awhile and help you get back in bed," he said.

I hadn't noticed but when I sat down, I rested my elbow on Carl's bed. I started to doze off when I felt Carl's cast touch my arm. His fingers protruded from the cast and he put them on top of mine. It was an act of intimacy that pleased me so that I looked up and saw that he was smiling at me. He took my arm, placed it under his top sheet and laid my palm on his cock. I had never touched anyone else's cock but mine and I was stunned. It felt so soft and silky. Carl started moving my hand so that it was stroking his cock in a masturbating fashion. I could feel his shaft hardening and I began to stroke him of my own volition. When it grew and hardened, I wrapped my whole hand around it and started jerking him off. His cock was massive. I could hardly encircle it, and a good two inches of it protruded beyond my hand. I don't know how long it had been since his last orgasm, but it seemed only seconds when he became short of breath, and then with a stifled whimper he came all over my hand and his foot cast.

He handed me a wad of tissues with his good hand. I cleaned up everything as best I could, and I threw the dirty tissues in the waste basket.

"Thank you Aaron," Carl said. "You have no idea how I needed that. I pretty much can't move, but maybe we can find a way for me to help you out."

Just then the nurse came back and helped me into bed. "If you'd like," he said, "I can help you take a real shower after your stitches are removed."

"I'd like that," I said.

I guess Carl and I were beginning to heal because we both finished the evening meal with nothing left over. My dessert had been a small tub of chocolate pudding. I even buzzed the nurse, whose name was Jorge by the way, and he got me a second pudding. He made us both as comfortable in bed as possible, gave us our evening meds, turned out our lights and bade us sleep well this evening. We watched TV for awhile until Carl said, "Let's talk."

He turned off the TV and asked, "Do you have a boy friend?"

I should have just said no and left it at that. I don't know what possessed me, but I decided to be honest with him.

"No," I answered. "Carl, I'm a virgin. I haven't even had the courage to walk into a gay bar. Maybe if I had someone to go with, but I don't know a soul in San Francisco, much less a gay soul. Your cock was the first one I ever touched other than my own."

"Wow," he said. "I didn't know. I hope I didn't scare you."

"No. It was wonderful."

"We have to find a way to take care of you," he said with determination in his voice.

"As wonderful as that sounds, that'll be tough."

"Not at all," he told me. "Jorge got you standing and walking a little. If you can just stand up and face my bed, I can do the rest."

"But that's the side with your arm cast," I pointed out to him, thinking he wanted to reciprocate by whacking me off.

"Let me worry about that," he said.

We waited until the lights were dimmed in the hallways and visiting hours were over. The ward seemed to be bathed in an eerie silence so different than the daytime hustle and bustle.

"Now," Carl said.

I was more afraid of pain than the inability to sit up and put my feet over the bed. I gritted my teeth and threw first one leg and then the other over the side of the bed. When I was in an upright position, I slid my butt further and further to the edge of the bed until my feet touched the floor. I pushed both my arms down on the bed and forced myself into a standing position. I felt a little stretching where I had stitches, but it was very mild and I didn't think that I was doing any damage. As soon as I was standing I supported myself by holding on to Carl's bed.

"Move up the bed until you are standing even with my head," he ordered. I did as he asked. It only took one little slide. He raised the top of his bed until his mouth was even with my cock. Then he slid the upper part of his body until his face was almost hanging off the bed.

"Take your cock out and put it in my mouth," he said. I only had to raise my hospital gown to expose myself, but I was so excited I just fumbled around. By the time I got the gown out of the way, I was fully erect. Carl gave a little whistle and said, "It's beautiful."

He started out by pushing back my foreskin with his tongue, and I remembered that he was not circumcised either. I helped by holding the retracted foreskin out of the way. His tongue licked all around my cock head and I became faint with pleasure. I leaned harder against the bed and further into him. After teasing me for awhile he took my seven inch rod into his mouth, a little at a time, until I could feel his chin on my balls. His pursed lips slid up and down my shaft and his tongue flicked up and down the underside of my cock.

I had dreamed of this happening to me a million times, but yet I was unprepared for the erotic pleasure he was affording me. I wanted to scream, but remembered where I was and stifled myself. Carl seemed to be lost in his own little dream world. For a second he took my cock out of his mouth and murmured, "This tastes so good."

He resumed sucking my cock and I felt my orgasm growing. I stuffed a fist into my mouth and with my other hand I pulled Carl's head hard into me. I came with as stifled a scream as I could manage, and was absolutely shocked that Carl swallowed every drop, and then made sure that there was nothing left. He held me inside him for a long while before releasing my limp prick.

"Thank you," he said. "That was absolutely wonderful."

When he said that, I realized that sucking cock could be as enjoyable as being sucked. That was a good thing to know. I bent down with some difficulty and for the first time in my life I kissed another man. His lips were warm and inviting and I loved the feel of his tongue when it entered my mouth. I believe that I even tasted some of my own cum which must have remained in his mouth. I was one happy dude until I realized that I couldn't climb back into the high hospital bed.

Carl buzzed for Jorge. "What's the problem?" he asked as he came into our room. When he saw us he started laughing. I think he sized up the situation immediately.

"Was it good for both of you?" he asked. He didn't wait for an answer but he said, "Next time call me first and I'll get you both into a comfortable position." He helped me into bed and we heard him laughing all the way down the hall.

The next morning, after all the hospital routines were completed, and Carl and I were as comfortable in bed as we were ever going to get, we received a visit from two very austere suits. They identified themselves as attorneys for the cruise line.

There were many platitudes offered to us about how sorry they were that this unfortunate incident occurred and for the distress it had caused us. They took out some papers and asked us to sign releases. It seems that the cruise company, in addition to paying all the hospital, hotel and air fare expenses, was offering us each $25,000 for these releases. To me that sounded like a small fortune, but Carl started to laugh.

"We've already consulted some local attorneys and they are thinking more in the neighborhood of one million bucks each. Good day gentlemen. You'll hear from them." Carl reached over to his bedside table which was on his good side and reached for a business card. "The name of the firm is Ridley, Ridley and Frankel." He replaced the card and turned his face away from the two attorneys.

One of them said, "We are only authorized to go to $400,000."

"Good day, gentlemen," Carl repeated and turned away again. The two men left.

"Are you crazy?" I asked when they were gone. That's a bloody fortune."

"Don't worry, Hotboy," Carl said. "We'll get at least $750,000 each. He called me by my screen name and then I remembered I had given it to him when I told him my story. He sensed what I was thinking, and said, "You are hot, you know." I looked over at him and he blew me a kiss. I found myself blushing, but I blew one back to him.

At about 11 AM, Dr. Berriman came into the room with one of the nurses. He removed my dressings and said, "You're looking good, young man." He then proceeded to remove my stitches. When they were gone, he bathed my surgical scars with an antiseptic solution and put on fresh bandages. "After tomorrow you won't need these," he said. "I'll probably discharge you the day after tomorrow so you can make arrangements to fly home."

Then he said to Carl, "Tomorrow morning, I'm changing your foot cast. It will be smaller and you'll be able to walk, well hobble, on it with crutches. The day after that, I'll have you taken to the hotel where the cruise line is putting you up until we remove the casts. How does that sound to you?"

"Great doc, just great," Carl answered him.

When the doctor left and we were alone, Carl looked at me. "Aaron," he said, we are both getting out of the hospital in two days. Why don't you stay with me in the hotel for a few days before flying home? Consider it part of your recovery process. You shouldn't go back to work for awhile anyway."

As he made this proposition to me, he raised his bed sheet to show me his massive raging hardon.

"It sounds good to me," I said, "But I told my boss I'd be home in a week, so why don't we plan on three or four days. I'll be waiting for you in San Francisco, I swear."

"It's a deal," he said to me and blew me another kiss.

That afternoon, the suits returned and offered us $750,000 each, just as Carl had predicted. This was in addition to all the costs of the trip and the hotel. My head was spinning so fast, I got nauseous. I thought Carl would grab the papers and sign right off, but instead he said, "Please leave the papers here and return tomorrow. We need to talk about it."

"Fair enough!" one of the lawyers said. We'll see you tomorrow bright and early."

As soon as they left, Carl turned to me and in a sing song manner said, "I told you so."

"Why did you tell them to come back?" I asked.

"We'll accept of course, but I wanted to make them sweat. $750,000 is nothing to them. Think about the millions they'll be paying out to the parents of those dead kids and to the family of that dead couple."

Both of us lay back in bed thinking about how our lives were about to change. Suddenly Carl said, "Hey we have got to take care of the airline tickets. We buzzed for the nurse, who helped us get the airline on the phone. When we explained that we had been hospitalized after that horrific bus crash, we were informed that there would be no charge for altering the flight arrangements. I rebooked the same flight I had, but for six days from now. Carl was left open ended until he was cleared for flying.

After dinner, Jorge asked me if I wanted a real shower. Is the Pope Catholic? He removed my dressings which were clean and showed no blood or drainage. Then he helped me out of bed which was so much easier with the stitches out. The shower was in the bathroom. It had no door or shower curtain, but plenty of handle bars. Jorge told me to step out of my slippers and gown as he adjusted the water temperature.

I stepped in and he handed me a wash cloth and a bar of soap. I began to wash my face and neck and then I soaped myself under the arms. From there I headed for my chest and cock and as I did so I automatically turned my back toward Jorge. I was still a shy Mormon boy.

"Give me the soap," he said "and I'll do your back." I handed him the soap and stepped back toward him as far as I could without leaving the shower. He began to wash my back and then he started to do my ass. I felt his fingers massaging my crack and I began to get hard. He inserted a soapy finger into my crack and found my prostate. "You like?" he asked.

"I like," I answered. Suddenly he wrapped his other hand around my cock and started stroking. With one finger up my ass and the other hand jerking me off, I came without even trying to stifle my scream.

"You can rinse off now," he said. He helped me out of the shower and he helped me dry myself. He brought me fresh slippers and a new gown and got me back into bed. He put on a new dressing and I was ready for the night.

As he left the room, Carl asked, "Hey Jorge, how about me?"

"Later," he said and was gone.

True to his word Jorge returned right after lights out. He woke us both and first gave Carl a blow job and then me.

I was beginning to think that a stay in the hospital was not such a bad thing.

- CHAPTER THREE -

Early in the morning on the day before our release from the hospital, the suits came to our room. We were each given a complete accounting. The amount of the check we would each receive would be just shy of $753,000. We both arranged for the checks to be electronically deposited into our checking accounts and we signed all the documents. The lawyers gave us each a copy of everything. We all shook hands and they left.

Shortly after that, two orderlies came in the room with a gurney and took Carl away. When he returned, his new arm cast covered only about three inches below his elbow and about four inches above it. His foot cast stopped about mid calf and had a rubber bar at the bottom. He was also given a pair of crutches. One of the orderlies said that one of the nurses would easily be able to cover the casts with plastic and help Carl take a real shower in a few hours. They wanted to make sure the cast was good and hard before he stood on it. Fortunately it was Jorge who did the honors late that afternoon. He played a little with Carl in the shower but whispered in Carl's ear that he was saving the best for after the lights went out on the ward.

Jorge came to our room after lights out. I told him that I was the only one of the three of us who had never tasted cock, and I sort of complained to him about it.

"I'll remedy that," he said. It was easy now for Carl to sit up in bed and drop his legs down over the side. Jorge got Carl into that position and then he sat right next to Carl on the bed so that their thighs were touching. He lifted Carl's gown exposing him and then he pushed down his pants and shorts, and he too was exposed.

"Go to it tiger," he commanded me. I had now reached a point where I slid easily off the bed. The chair was still between the two beds. I sat down on it. Carl was closest and I leaned forward and took him in my mouth. Carl sensed my inexperience and started telling me what to do. I could not believe how good cock tasted. I was sailing on clouds. I followed his instructions faithfully and soon he was moaning loudly. He pushed me away and said, "I don't want to cum yet. Work on Jorge." I happily obliged.

Jorge was not about to stop me like Carl did. He had to get back to work. He came rather quickly amidst stifled screams, and he shot several spasms into my waiting mouth. I swallowed every last drop. Jorge got himself together and told me to work on my buddy. Who was I to argue? Now Carl abandoned himself to his passion and came quickly in my mouth. This time I didn't swallow all of it and passed some on to Carl, who avidly devoured his own cum.

Carl never moved from his position at the edge of the bed, but he told me to stand up and face him. By now I knew what to do. I took my cock in hand and maneuvered it into his mouth and he transported me to the Garden of Eden. He did a really good job of swallowing it all, so we were both relatively clean. But just the same I went into the bathroom and wet a wash cloth and wiped us both up. Carl let me wipe his cock and balls and we both giggled as I did it.

"I have to pee," he announced. I buzzed for Jorge, who helped him stand up with the crutches. Jorge instructed him how to hop on his good leg and swing his bad one. After peeing, Carl decided to "walk" up and down the hall to practice, and I accompanied him. I was pleased to note that we were both getting our strength back.

When we were ready to turn in for the night, I got Carl into bed, and I leaned down and kissed him. Our kisses lasted a long time. They were sloppy and sensuous.

"Tomorrow we'll be alone in the hotel," he whispered in my ear. "How great is that? This cruise is turning out to be better than I ever dreamed."

I think that sometimes the gay community can be one big support group. Carl was approved for the hotel room by the cruise line, but I was expected to return home upon my discharge from the hospital. Therefore, Carl was to be transmitted to the hotel by ambulance, but I needed a cab, presumably to take me to the airport. I was very pleasantly surprised when Jorge told me that he would come over before his shift and drive me to the hotel. Carl and I looked forward to three days of bliss.

Before going off duty that night, Jorge came to say goodbye to Carl in case he was discharged before he came to get me. They kissed each other and Carl whispered something in Jorge's ear. He was inviting him to come to his hotel room whenever he could, during and after my stay. I don't know why, but that raised a spark of jealousy in me.

My suitcase and my meager belongings had been destroyed in the crash, but miraculously Carl's had been salvaged. We were about the same height and build and he lent me some clothes to wear, but his shoes didn't fit. On the way to the hotel, Jorge stopped at a shoe store and I had no hesitation using my credit card to buy a pair of sneakers and some crew socks.

Not surprisingly, Jorge valet parked his car and helped me up to Carl's room. He had time for a three way session with us before he went on duty. Carl opened the door, and told us to come in quickly. He was naked and was hopping around on one crutch. It wasn't long before the three of us were getting comfortable in the big king size bed.

Carl was the least mobile of the three of us. We put him on his back and told him to just lie back and enjoy himself as Jorge and I sucked his cock together. Then Jorge introduced me to a new sensation. He told me to squat between Carl's legs and suck Carl's cock. As soon as I was doing that, Jorge came up behind me, spread my ass cheeks and started sucking my ass. I could feel his tongue pry open my ass hole and I swear it felt better than a blow job. I could hear Jorge tear something open and I knew what was going to happen. He was putting on a rubber and he was going to fuck me. Jorge was only about six inches hard, but still nothing had ever been up there before and I was scared. To get my mind off it I sucked Carl harder and harder. His body was contorting with pleasure as best it could with his casts and all.

I felt Jorge's tongue leave my ass and his cockhead press against the entrance to my tunnel of love. Jorge was not delicate. He pushed right in to the hilt and I screamed in pain. He did not withdraw, but held perfectly still instead. Little by little the pain subsided and was replaced by pangs of pure pleasure. I began to make little whimpering sounds and Jorge began to stroke in and out very slowly. After awhile I could hear his breathing become labored and he began to pump harder. I yelled at him, "Faster, harder, faster, harder!" His cock was stroking my prostate and I could not stop my orgasm which was building quickly.

Then it happened. Jorge came screaming. Spasm after spasm filled his condom with cum. Immediately after that, I came all over the bed sheet. As if he were miles away I heard Carl say, "Please fuck me like that later." And then his juices gushed into my mouth.

After we recovered, we put plastics on Carl's casts and we all showered together. The hotel shower was large enough for four big guys. When Jorge left, Carl said, "Please come by any time." Again a strange, unexplained jealousy came over me.

Carl and I spent the next three days mostly lying naked together in bed. Jorge only came over one more time on his day off and he didn't stay very long. I sensed that he was saving it all for Carl when I left. The only time I left Carl's naked side was the first day after Jorge left. I went downstairs and went shopping. I bought a small suitcase and some shirts, slacks, a belt, socks, shoes and toiletries. I shopped as quickly as possible so that I could return to my love nest.

We ordered all our meals from room service. When it was delivered, I always hid in the bathroom and when the maid came, I left the room before her arrival and waited in the lobby until she was finished. Carl and I made love constantly. Neither of us knew we had it in us. We explored our bodies and every one of their openings in every way we could think of. We were not afraid to try anything that occurred to us. If I had ever been reticent about anything, I lost it in the tropical Florida air.

I had to be at the airport by 4 PM on the day of my departure. Before I left, Carl and I clung together. It was all we could do to let go of each other, and yet I was disturbed knowing that Jorge would be sharing this bed for at least the next three weeks. Finally, I gave him one final kiss and ran out of the room.

My flight arrived only ten minutes late. I didn't have to go to baggage claim because the small suitcase I bought was designed to fit in the overhead compartment. As I exited the security area, I heard my name called and there was Brad. Why had I never seen how handsome he was? My heart skipped a beat and another unexplained feeling came over me. I was suddenly consumed with guilt. But why did I feel that way? Carl and I had not made any commitments to each other, and weren't he and Jorge going to be fucking each other crazy for the next three or four weeks?

Brad grabbed my suitcase, placed it on the ground and proceeded to kiss me gently. "I don't want to hurt you," he said. "Tell me if I'm hurting you." He didn't wait for an answer but resumed kissing me on the lips in this very public place. Well, we were in San Francisco. This kind of kissing was common place.

On the way to his car, I said to him, "I had no idea you felt this way about me. How did you know I was gay, and why have you waited this long to let me know how you felt?"

"I really don't know. I just know I fell in love with you the day I hired you. How did I know you were gay? When you told me the name of your cruise line and the ship you were on, I knew it was a gay cruise."

"Of course," I said, "how stupid of me."

"Look," he said, "I don't want you to be alone for awhile. Would you stay with me for a few days at least?"

My mind began to race. Carl would be calling me in an hour or two. I didn't want to be at Brad's place when he called. On the other hand, if I stayed with Brad, I knew we would have sex, and I wanted to make love to Brad very badly.

I'd really like to go home tonight and get settled back in, and I'd like to go to work tomorrow," I said. Brad looked so unhappy that I said something I never intended to say. "Why don't you stay with me tonight and maybe I'll stay with you for awhile after that?" Brad grinned from ear to ear.

"It's a deal," he said.

They hadn't fed us anything on the plane and I suddenly realized that I was hungry. When I told Brad that I was starving, he stopped at our Wendy's and we had free hamburgers, fries and a drink and then he took me home.

My room smelled musty and I opened the window. Brad was very silent, but he kept smiling at me. He haltingly asked me if I still hurt or could I have sex. He looked so shy when he asked me that question, that my heart melted and I took him in my arms and kissed him.

"I'm fine," I said, "I'm good to go. But I feel grungy from the trip. How about showering with me and I'll show you my scars?" We both laughed and were undressed in a second. We stood and looked at each other. We were both as hard as a rock, and both about seven inches long. We were about the same size around, but Brad was cut and I wasn't. Brad took me in his arms and crushed our cocks together.

"My dreams are coming true," he whispered to me.

I had never dreamed of Brad in a sexual way, until he kissed me at the airport when I was leaving for the cruise. I wished desperately that I could say the same thing to him, but I couldn't lie. Just then the phone rang. I knew it was Carl, and I rushed to pick up the phone.

"Hi handsome," Carl said, "I just called to make sure you got home OK. Jorge took two sick days off, and he's taken your place in bed so don't worry if you don't hear from me for a few days. Take care." Bingo! Just like that he hung up. I was very disappointed, but at the same time I was somehow relieved.

"Who was that?" Brad asked.

"His name is Carl Gilmore. We shared a room at the hospital. He and I were going on the same cruise and he won't be coming home for another three or four weeks. You'll be delighted at the coincidence, but he manages a Burger King here in San Francisco."

"Great," Brad said. "I'd like to meet him when he gets home. I'm jealous that he shared a room with you for so long."

"Not to worry. Most of his body was in a cast, and he was pretty incapacitated," I lied. "Now how about that shower?"

We went into my tiny shower together. It was a really tight fit, but we didn't mind. The soap in the shower had gotten pretty dried up and I had to really wet it good to get suds out of it again. We took turns washing each other. I had lost all my shyness with Carl and got it all back with Brad. I kept missing all his erogenous areas. Finally he took the soap from me and started working on my balls. Then his hand engulfed my cock and he started stroking it. He teased my cock awhile and then he began to soap my ass. He wasn't shy about letting a finger or two slip in. All the while he was kissing me gently. His tongue found mine and slipped across it as light as a feather. It was intoxicating, and I gladly returned the pleasure. Carl's kisses had been rough and penetrating. Brad's tongue gave me new sensations. The shower was too small for further exploration of our bodies, so we dried ourselves and went into my twin size bed. Now that was a pretty tight fit also.

Brad seemed determined to take the helm. He was four years older than I, and he was my boss, so I guess he thought he had the right. He put me on my back and lay prone on top of me, but he didn't feel heavy at all. Our cocks were rubbing together and Brad was treating my tongue to his feathery tongue caresses. Then he began to slip down my body as his tongue explored my entire torso from neck to abdomen. When he reached each nipple, he suckled it and I began to moan. He kissed my belly button and darted his tongue into it. I had never trimmed my pubic hair and it was pretty bushy, but he began to kiss my pubic area just the same. Then he told me to roll over.

He started at my neck and kissed his way down my entire back until he reached my southern cheeks. He licked and kissed them both and then his tongue found my single crack. He ran his tongue up and down the crack until my ass hole began to open involuntarily, seeking his tongue. Eventually he let his tongue wander in and again his touch was light and feathery. Jorge's tongue had been rough as it forced its way in. My mind kept recording all the differences between Brad and Jorge and Carl.

Brad seemed to sense when I could bear it no longer and told me to turn over again. He squatted between my legs and cupped my balls in his hand, kneading them gently. I wanted to cum and he stopped so that I could recover. After waiting a bit, he leaned over and began to run his tongue up and down my shaft. I pulled back my foreskin and he began to swish his tongue around my sensitive head. I had to beg him to stop and concentrate on the shaft. Again he let my impending orgasm subside. Finally he took my entire prick into his mouth. He did this slowly and it was awhile before I felt his chin on my balls. He pursed his lips around the base of my cock and let his tongue bathe my shaft in an up and down stroking motion. His pursed lips moved slightly up and down, but his tongue was doing most of the work. When my balls began to shrink, he stopped and let me recover again.

"I need to cum," I whimpered.

"I know," he said, "just be patient."

He got out of bed and got something out of his trouser pocket. It was a lubricated condom which he removed and rolled down my aching, throbbing cock. Then he straddled me, reached behind his back and grabbed my cock. He placed the head at the opening to his love canal, and slowly and gently sat down on me. It seemed like several minutes before he was all the way in and I could feel his hairless ass on my body. He started a stroking motion. Instinctively, I started a counter motion, moving in the opposite direction from his thrusts. The effect was blowing my mind. I was totally in outer space, but I wasn't far enough out there, not to be aware that sex with Carl had never been this good. Yet, I had to remember that Carl's casts had to be very inhibiting. But then lightening struck me. Brad's main concern was to give me ultimate pleasure. Carl wanted only to be pleasured. What pleasure I derived with Carl, came only from his own needs, not mine.

"I'm cumming," I yelled at Brad and he thrust all the harder. I could feel my spunk filling the condom and rolling out the sides onto my pubic hair, but Brad did not stop thrusting until I had to beg him. He sat still on me, not moving, until my limp dick started to fall out. It finally did, leaving most of the wet condom inside of him. I reached around and pulled it out of his ass.

Brad was still sitting on top of me. He leaned over and placed his lips on mine. Once again his gentle tongue flicked over mine. Whenever he did that I became heady. I tried to tongue him harder, but he retained that sensuous way of kissing me.

He stopped kissing me for a moment and whispered in my ear. "I love you Aaron. I want you. I need you. Please love me back."

- Chapter Four -

"Please love me back," Brad pleaded.

I couldn't answer him, so I held him tight and put his head on my chest. I could feel his tears wetting my skin. I was in terrible turmoil. Brad loved me, but I didn't love him. I liked him a lot, but it just wasn't love. I loved Carl, even though I was well aware that he did not love me. I was certain that Carl viewed me as just another fuck buddy.

I thought that maybe when he got home and Jorge was out of the picture, he might come to realize that he loved me. Even as I prayed for that to happen, I knew it was wishful thinking. A good looking guy like Carl, with a cock that big, must have a zillion fuck buddies.

I ran my hand through Brad's hair and whispered in his ear, "I need time, Brad. This is all so new to me."

I held him closer and could feel his hard cock rubbing against my body. I realized that Brad had not been satisfied. Gently, I laid him down on the bed. My tongue found his nipples and I began to suck on them and then I worked my way down to his cock. I found his cock and his balls and used every lesson Carl and Jorge had instructed me in. I wanted to give Brad as much pleasure as he had given me. When I enveloped his cock in my mouth, I knew I had accomplished my goal from the way he writhed and moaned in absolute abandoned joy. Each time I felt his orgasm coming, I pulled off him and let him recover. I did this several times until finally he begged, "Let me cum Aaron. I can't stand it any more."

I lost count of the number of spasms he emptied in my mouth. I do know that I couldn't take all of his jism. A good deal was dribbling down my chin. I offered it to Brad who greedily drank it down.

The two of us lay still and exhausted on the bed. We rolled toward each other and wrapped our arms around one another. Then we fell asleep.

When I awoke, I had to pee badly. I carefully removed Brad's arms and went to the bathroom. On the way, I checked the time. It was 7 AM. The store opened at 6 AM and Brad was always there to open up. I peed quickly and went to rouse Brad.

"It's OK," he said. "I was hoping to spend the night with you so I asked Tommy to open up. I told him I didn't know what time I could get in, but it wouldn't be early."

"I really would like to go to work today," I said.

"No way, man! I won't let you. I don't want to see you at the store until your regular single shift on Monday. Anyway, I want you to save your strength for me."

I started to protest, but I knew it wouldn't be any use. Then again, I could use the time off. Three quarters of a million dollars was a lot to manage and I had to start managing. I needed the time off to make arrangements.

Brad eventually got up and said he had to go home and change before he went to work. He told me to pack my small bag and to be ready at 5 PM, when he would pick me up to go to his apartment.

I had no food in the house. I could have walked over to my Wendy's for a free breakfast, but I thought better of the idea, and I went to a nearby Denny's instead. On the way home, I stopped and did some food shopping.

After I put my groceries away, I called my bank and confirmed that my balance was in excess of $753,000. I walked over to the bank, which I knew had a financial investment division and asked to speak to an advisor. The receptionist looked at me and saw a teen ager. With her nose pointed straight up in the air, she asked me if I had an account with the bank and I answered affirmatively.

"May I have your account number," she asked me as if it was a great effort on her part. She looked at the computer screen and did a double take. She was no youngster and she should have known by now that you can't judge a book by its cover.

"Oh yes, Mr. Jackson," she said with a lilt in her voice. "I'll get someone right away." I expected her to buzz someone, but instead she ran into one of the offices, presumably to give the financial advisor a head's up.

A slightly chubby, but very handsome man, about forty-five years old, and about 5'8" came out of the office. He extended his hand to greet me and ushered me into his office.

"It's a pleasure to meet you, sir," he said. "I'm Larry Reilly."

SIR! Nobody had ever called me that before. I liked it.

"What can I do for you?" he asked.

"You can help me invest my money wisely," I said. "Don't bother with anything hairy," I instructed. "I want safe and sound investments, and if I'm not worth more a year from now than I am worth today, I'll take my money elsewhere." I have no idea where this assertiveness came from, but I didn't want him to think I was a pushover who he could take advantage of.

Before he could say anything, I added, "I want to keep about $1,000.00 in my checking account and I want to buy certificates of deposit up to the government insured maximum. I look to you to help me invest the rest, and remember, only solid investments, nothing risky."

"You're very young," he said. "With someone your age, who is as conservative as you are, I have my own little formula. I like to put about

40% into the stock market in solid dividend paying companies. I put about 25% into triple A bonds and about 15% in Preferred Stock. I like to put the balance into growth stocks. You know, emerging companies, maybe some foreign stuff. I promise you I won't invest in anything risky, just promising. How does that sound?"

Actually it sounded good to me, and in my most mature and professional manner, I asked. "How soon can you come up with a portfolio for me? I'd like to move on this as soon as possible. My money isn't earning anything right now and might as well be under the mattress."

"May I call you Aaron?" he asked me. I nodded. "It's a pleasure to deal with such a mature young man. Please call me Larry. I promise you that I'll work my ass off for you and you won't be sorry. Let's get some of the money working right away. I'll transfer $100,000.00 into CD's immediately at our highest and most preferred rate. Tell me. Do you want your interest and dividends reinvested or deposited to your checking account?"

That was a tough question. I hadn't thought about that. "Why don't we put it in my checking account." I answered. "I want to use some of it for living expenses. When the balance gets too high, I'll see you about investing the excess." Then as an afterthought I added, "Or maybe I'd like to buy a car or something."

"That's a plan," Larry said. "Now can I take you to lunch? It's just about that time.

I liked Larry a lot. He made me feel that he was competent to take care of my money. "Sure," I said. "That would be nice."

At the restaurant, which was too fancy for what I was wearing, Larry asked me to tell him something about myself. He thought it might help in his decision making process. I was so comfortable with him, that I decided to tell him everything from my excommunication to the bus accident and its financial consequences. All the while I was narrating my tale, he just stared at me in amazement and said nothing. I decided to skip my sex life, which had gone from nothing to running on all cylinders in a very short space of time.

When I was finished Larry reached into his wallet. With great pride and I think a lump in his throat, he showed me a picture of himself with a very distinguished looking, also forty something gentlemen. He was a good looking man and appeared to be tall and lean as opposed to Larry's portliness. The two men had their arms on each other's shoulders and were smiling broadly at the camera.

"This is my partner, Chuck," he said. "We've been together for twenty-four years. We'll be making a twenty-fifth anniversary party in about six months and you're invited. Do you have a boy friend to bring with you?"

I was astounded to learn that Larry was gay. Don't ask me why, but I decided to seek Larry's non-financial advice on my love life. I related to him the part of my story I had held back on. I admitted that Carl did not love me, but I loved him, that Brad loved me, but I didn't love him. "What I can't understand," I told him, "is that Brad is a hundred times better lover than Carl."

"What do you mean?" he asked me.

"Well, Brad wants only to give me pleasure and Carl wants to use me for his own pleasure. Does that make sense?"

"It certainly does, Aaron. From the sound of it, I would suggest you see a lot of Brad. He loves you a lot and maybe if you don't love the man right away you will learn to love his attributes."

"Well, he's my boss," I answered, "so I will see a lot of him. It's when Carl comes home in a few weeks that I'm worried about."

"See how it plays out," Larry said. "I'm here for you whenever you need me." He picked up the check and put his credit card on it. The waiter came and picked up the card, and then walked off.

"How about you come and see me tomorrow at about 1 PM. I should have a complete plan of action for you by then." I nodded my head.

"By the way," he asked, "why are you continuing to work at Wendy's?"

"I really don't know," I answered sincerely. "I don't particularly want anyone to know that I've come into money. The only thing I might do is move into a real apartment."

"Good idea," Larry said. He started to shake my hand, but instead he pulled me to him and gave me a hug. "Your parents are fucking fools," he said. "They have no idea what a fine young man they threw out. If I had a son, I'd want him to be you."

I don't know why, but I had the feeling that Larry had just adopted me. The future would prove that he and his partner, Chuck Harrington, had indeed adopted me, not legally, but in spirit. In time they would come to fill the void my parents had left in my life, and I was the better off for it. I left Larry with the certain conviction that I had put myself in good hands.

Brad picked me up promptly at 5 PM. When we arrived at his apartment building, the address sounded familiar. I looked in my wallet. Carl had written down his local address and telephone number for me. As incredible as it sounds, he lived in this very building in apartment 2C. Brad was in 3C. I involuntarily muttered, "Oh no."

"What's wrong?" Brad asked.

"Nothing, nothing at all," I lied.

From the moment Brad picked me up, I tried to look at him in a new light. Larry told me to try to love his attributes. During the evening, I found out how easy that was. He was so careful not to harm my healing body in any way. He wouldn't let me do even the simplest tasks. I watched him as he prepared a gourmet dinner for us. "No Wendy's for us tonight," he informed me.

He baked two Cornish hens, which he served with oven roasted potatoes and green beans. As an appetizer we had shrimp cocktail and for dessert, strawberry shortcake with coffee. While the chickens were baking in the oven, he opened a bottle of red wine, and we made a toast, "To us." That made me a little uncomfortable.

During the course of the preparation of the meal and during the time we ate it, Brad would come over and give me his wonderful kisses. His feathery tongue would glide over mine and I tingled all over. I couldn't help wonder what was wrong with me. He was treating me like visiting royalty and all I had in mind was Carl's return. I was a fool. I knew it, and I couldn't do a thing about it. In fact, I was so disturbed that I told Brad that I ached a lot tonight and was afraid to get too physical.

"That's fine," he said. "Don't worry about it." We fell asleep hugging each other and just fondling our cocks. Brad made me feel like I was in a womb, warm and safe, and still I could only think of Carl. I was convinced that I was one sick puppy.

In the morning I asked Brad to take me home and pick me up again after work. I had resolved that tonight I was going to make Brad the happiest lover on planet Earth. When I got home, I cleaned the apartment, and did a laundry. At lunch time, I went to Wendy's. Brad was very discreet and did not show me any affection, but the rest of my co-workers were glad to see me and some showed it physically by hugging me. Brad warned them not to hurt me. It killed me that he always had my welfare at heart and my only thoughts were of Carl.

I took a salad tray and Brad took a hamburger. We went into his office to eat lunch and he closed the door. As soon as the door was closed, I grabbed him and started to kiss him passionately. At the same time I lightly grabbed his package and when I heard him moan, I stopped.

"That's it for now," I said. "You get the rest tonight." He smiled so broadly at me that I registered another attribute. He had a beautiful smile.

After lunch I headed to the bank for my 1 PM appointment with Larry. When I went into his office, he closed the door and embraced me warmly.

"How are you feeling today, son?" he asked me. He said 'son' the way an older man addresses a younger one. He meant nothing by it, but I jokingly answered, "Just fine, Dad."

We smiled at each other and guess what? After that he always called me son, and I always called him Dad. We had officially adopted each other.

"Before we start," Larry said, "I want you to know that after you said you might want to buy a car, and maybe get a nicer apartment, I put $50,000.00 in a money market account, so you would have ready access to cash. The interest rate is low, but you can draw on it readily without disturbing other investments."

Larry took a bunch of computer generated papers from his desk and laid them out for me. He started to explain what he planned for me, but I laid my hand on his and said, "Dad, I don't really understand any of this. I trust you totally to act in my best interests. Just tell me what to do."

What I had to do was sign a bunch of documents giving Larry my power of attorney to act as my financial agent in all matters related to my accounts with the bank. I signed the papers and we shook hands in a business like manner. Then Larry embraced me, but the embrace was somehow different than previously. It was like a father embracing a loving son. I didn't want to, but I started to cry and when I looked at Larry he was crying too.

"Look son," Larry said. "Tomorrow is Friday. Chuck and I would really like you to come for dinner. You can bring whoever you want, but I would hope that you bring Brad. By the way have you been studying his attributes?"

"Yes," I said. "He's kind, considerate, patient, loving, sweet, handsome, a great lover, a fantastic cook, and if that isn't enough, he has the most beautiful smile in the world."

"I can see that you don't like him," Larry said jokingly. He wrote his home address and telephone number on a piece of paper and said, "We'll expect you abut six. I hope you will bring Brad too"

When Brad came to pick me up, I was brimming with excitement. "I have something to tell you," I said. Without telling him about my money, I said, "I have become very friendly with one of the men who works at my bank. He's an older guy, and he and his partner have invited me to dinner tomorrow evening. He's kind of acting like I was the son he never had or something. They want me to bring a friend so I was wondering if you would like to go with me."

"Are you kidding?" Brad asked. "I'd love to go with you. It would be like we were a real couple going to dinner at the house of another real couple. I'd like that very much."

Brad was excited for us to be doing something as a 'real couple.' I winced at the thought. I just didn't want to be a couple, not even with Carl, and I truly believed that I loved Carl.

"You're not making dinner tonight," I said. "I'm taking you out for being so nice to me."

"No, no," Brad said. "I can't let you spend money on me."

"Forget about it," I said. "No is not an option. I took him to an inexpensive Italian restaurant where the food was good and plentiful. I even bought a bottle of wine over Brad's objection. I couldn't help wondering if Carl would have objected as Brad had.

That night in bed, I lived up to the promise I made. I told Brad that he was not to make love to me tonight. I was going to make love to him and give him the most pleasure that I was capable of giving.

I sucked his cock, teasing it until he was crying for relief. Then I put a lubricated condom on his cock and I sat on it. When I had him in me all the way, I just sat still. He tried to move up and down but I held him down. After a while I moved up and down on him always stopping in time to make sure he didn't cum. When I tortured him enough, I let him cum. He filled the condom, and much of his spunk flowed out the sides, just as mine had done. I began to wonder how it would feel to have his cum fill me up, and I decided to ask him if we could be tested so we could stop using a condom.

I must have been crazy to think of that. If I said anything like that, Brad would deduce, and rightly so, that I wanted us to be exclusive. No way was I ready for that. I yearned for Carl so badly.

Friday evening Brad drove us to Larry and Chuck. We stood at the front door with a bottle of wine as a house gift. For the life of me I could not understand why I was apprehensive about going in. It was Brad who rang the bell.

Almost immediately, the door was opened by Chuck. The picture didn't lie. He was about 6 feet tall, very lean, and very distinguished looking.

"You must be Aaron," he said looking straight at me. Then discreetly, he looked at Brad and asked, "And who might you be?" There was no doubt about it. He sighed a sigh of relief when Brad said, "I'm Bradley, sir."

Chuck held out his hand and said to Brad, "I'm Chuck." Larry appeared out of nowhere with an apron on. He grabbed me and kissed me on the lips. "Welcome, welcome son and you too, Brad."

At the sound of the word, son, Brad looked at me quizzically. I know he was thinking that it was awfully intimate for my banker to call me *son*. So fully aware of what I was doing, I said, "It's a pleasure to be here *Dad*."

Chuck asked what we would like to drink, and Brad and I answered in one voice, "Just coke, if you have it, Chuck." We started to laugh and Brad said, "Bread and butter." *Shit*, I thought, *there's another thing we have in common,* and of course, that disturbed me. Carl why aren't you here to unconfuse me?

Larry and Chuck had prepared a very simple meal. They barbequed steaks which they served with baked potatoes. The only drinks they put on the table were water and bottles of soda. The appetizer was a simple lettuce wedge with an assortment of dressings. For dessert we had apple pie ala mode with coffee.

After dinner we sat around and chatted. Conversation flowed comfortably. You would think that we were four old friends who had known each other forever. Larry was the epitome of discretion. He never mentioned anything about our financial arrangement.

At one point Brad asked our hosts how they had met. "I'm a hopeless romantic," he informed everyone, looking straight at me, "and I need to know these things."

For some reason I assumed that Larry would relate the story, but it turned out to be Chuck who began to speak.

"I had just landed a position at Berkeley teaching English Lit. All I had was a furnished studio apartment. I did not know a single person in Frisco and I was feeling sorry for myself. I'm not a drinker and I'm not much for bars. I thought about going to a gay bar, but was too shy to go alone. (I laughed inwardly at that last statement.) Anyway, one evening I went to the Library at the University just to pass some time.

"I think Larry is hot now, but you should have seen him twenty-five years ago. I sat down at a table with a book, I can't remember what it was, and there was Larry across the table from me. Gentlemen, for me it was love at first sight. I wanted desperately to meet this guy. I didn't care if he was straight or gay, and I just shed all my shyness and asked right out, 'Hey man, what are you studying there?'

'I'm working on my senior thesis in finance,' he answered without even looking up. So I persisted.

'I'm going to be teaching English Lit here next semester. I just moved here from Illinois. I don't know a soul here and I think I might go crazy before school starts.'

Finally, Larry looked up and into my eyes. He smiled at me and I wanted to grab him and make love to him right there in the library. 'I'm Larry Reilly,' he said extending his hand.

'Chuck Harrington,' I said, shaking his hand. How good, how right, his hand felt in mine. He smiled at me and I knew he felt the same way.

'I'm about done here for now,' Larry said. 'Would you like to have a cup of coffee with me?'

"That was it," Chuck continued. "He came back to my furnished studio and we made love. We haven't been apart one night ever since."

In a way that was very atypical of me, I jumped up and embraced Chuck first, and then Larry. "Thanks for sharing," I said.

After that there was an uncomfortable silence for a few minutes until Chuck said to me, "Look son, if you are going to call Larry Dad, you have to call me Dad also."

"I'm flattered," I said, "but that's confusing. How about if I call you Pop, and you can call me Son." After that I had a dad and a pop and they both had a son.

Brad was silent through all of this. He was usually very upbeat and buoyant and his silence confused me. On the way back to his apartment he said, "You know how jealous I am. I want so much to be a part of your family."

"Please Brad," I literally pleaded. "I like you a lot, but please don't pressure me."

- CHAPTER FIVE -

On Sunday, Brad and I made love all afternoon in my apartment, but I asked him to go home and get a good night's sleep. He needed to open the store, and I had to be at work by 6:00 AM the next morning before the store opened.

I was lying in bed and brooding. I had not heard from Carl all weekend. It was three hours later in Ft. Lauderdale and I thought it was too late to call, but I vowed to call his hotel first thing in the morning. Given the time difference it would be just the right time to call.

It was 5:30 AM on the west coast when I called. The desk clerk informed me that Carl Gilmore had checked out. I was confused. The cruise line was paying for all his expenses, and he was supposed to stay there until his casts were removed. If Carl had a cell phone, I didn't know the number.

On my first break of the morning, I called the Burger King where Carl worked. I asked if anyone there had heard from him, and I was informed that they didn't expect him back for another few weeks. I was beside myself with worry. Brad could see how agitated I was and he wanted to know what was wrong.

"Nothing!" I snapped at him, and he backed off. Somehow I got through the day. Brad wanted to take me home, but I told him that I didn't want any company today, and he reluctantly left me and went home. He looked so terribly sad, and I didn't even care.

When I got home, I found a letter slipped under my door. I could see that it was certified and a return receipt had been requested. My landlord had signed the receipt. I saw immediately that it was from Carl and I ripped it open. As I did so, something fell out of the envelope and on to the floor. It was a key.

I began to read:

Hi Aaron:

It should not come as a surprise to you that Jorge and I have something special going on here. I am checking out of the hotel and moving in with him. I will not be returning to San Francisco.

This morning I called my landlord's rental agent and authorized him to get a mover to pack up the stuff in my apartment and move it down to Florida. I am on a month to month tenancy and I sent him two months rent with my notice. The movers were instructed that they will be paid at the other end.

I am enclosing the key to my car. I would appreciate it if you would find it on my parking lot. The registration is in the glove compartment. It's a 1997 blue Chevy with plates CRT23FX. Take it to any used car dealer and get what you can for it. If you can't sell it, just abandon it. If you do sell it, keep the money for your effort.

My address here is: c/o Jorge Rodriguez, 1793 NW 23 Ave, Apt. 2B, Ft. Lauderdale FL 33043. The phone number is 954-555-5833.

Just to fill you in on what has been happening. I am buying a condo for cash. It's right on the ocean in an upscale strip called Galt Ocean Drive. I stole it for $425,000.00. I figure furnishings will be another $50,000.00. As soon as the deal goes through, I'll send you the address and the telephone number. Of course, Jorge *will be moving in with me. I also bought me some wheels. It's a 2009 Jaguar two seater, convertible sports car. That set me back $89,000, but what a beauty. Jorge and I went on a shopping spree and we both look like Palm Beach money. As soon as my casts are off, we are going on an eighteen day cruise. How cool is that? Oh yes, Jorge quit his job.*

When I get all settled down in the condo, I'll contact you again. Maybe you can visit us sometime. We can have those great old three ways.

Hugs, Carl

I was stunned. I started to cry. It was quite possible that I would never see Carl again. I cried for at least an hour and didn't have any dinner. At about 8 PM the phone rang. It was Brad. I told him that I couldn't talk to anyone just now and to please leave me alone. I knew that I had wounded him and I couldn't stop myself. I would have hurt him more if I could, but I just hung up on him. I didn't want Brad in my life and why couldn't he see that?

I fell asleep curled up in a fetal position, crying like a baby. I was awakened some time later by the harsh sound of my door bell. I was groggy but looked at the clock hanging over my sink. In the moonlight, which filled the room, I could see that it was a minute before midnight.

"Who is it?" I asked sounding drunk. I wished I was drunk.

"It's Brad. Open up. I'm really worried about you."

"Go away. I don't want to see you, ever again."

He began to bang on my door. "You'd better open up. I'm just going to stand here and bang on your door until I wake up every one of your neighbors."

Reluctantly, I opened the door. He rushed in, closed the door, and tried to embrace me. I turned my face away from him.

"Who hurt you like this?" he asked. "I'll kill him."

"Fat chance," I said. "He's in Florida. Believe me if he was here, I'd kill him myself."

Suddenly I started to cry again. "I'm such a fucking fool," I said. "I knew he had no feelings for me beyond having sex with me, but I kept hoping."

"There is someone I didn't know about?" Brad asked me, sounding sad and stunned at the same time. He got up to leave, but I grabbed his arm.

"Please stay," I begged. "I really need a friend right now. I should actually be talking to Larry and Chuck, but I have no wheels and it's too late to call them."

Brad sat down on my bed and his head dropped almost to his knees. I took Carl's letter from the kitchen table and sat down next to Brad. "Here, read this," I said to him.

As he read, Brad's face got more confused. "I don't understand," he said. "You told me that Carl was your hospital room mate and nothing more. If he manages a Burger King, where is he getting all this money from? And who is this Jorge who has apparently stolen him from you? You have to fill me in."

I lay down on my bed. Brad was sitting on the edge and I did not invite him to lie down with me. I was surprised because I wanted him next to me desperately, but it just didn't seem right at the moment. Still, I needed to do something to show him that I did care for him so I took his hand in mine.

"It's a long story," I told him. "Are you sure you have the time?"

Then Brad said something which sounded very harsh but so wonderful at the same time. "I love you, you idiot. Whatever time represents the rest of my life, it's available to you."

I was really touched and I mumbled, "Thank you."

"Now talk," he said and he began to stroke my hair.

"I was in and out of consciousness for about the first week after the accident. As I began to heal and as they began to remove the drainage tubes, the doctor ordered that the nurses get me out of bed and start walking me around. Jorge was my evening nurse. One evening he got me out of bed. I was exhausted immediately, and he sat me on a chair between my bed and Carl's. I was dozing off when Carl took my hand and placed it on his cock. He indicated that he would like me to masturbate him. It was the first time I had ever felt another man's cock and when he came, it made quite a mess. I wiped it up as best I could. Later that night, when the lights were out, I worked my way out of bed and stood at Carl's bedside. He gave me my first blow job and it was wonderful.

"After all the tubes and stitches were removed, Jorge gave me my first shower, he played with me and got me off and later on, he and Carl sat at the edge of Carl's bed and they taught me how to give them each blow jobs. When we were discharged, Carl was placed in a hotel until his casts would be removed and the doctors said he could fly home. Instead of coming straight home, I spent three days with Carl. Occasionally Jorge joined us in a three way. Looking back on it now, I did usually feel like a third wheel."

Brad was silent when I stopped talking, but then he said, "Carl didn't ever love you, honey. Obviously he was falling for Jorge. You were a convenient boy toy."

"I know," I said. "Compared to you, he has no character at all. Yet I fell in love and I couldn't shake him. I simply pushed you aside, because I wanted him so badly. I'm sorry, but I just don't love you. I love Carl and I know what love feels like."

I could tell that Brad was hurt. He got off the bed and sat on a chair.

"Tell me about the money," he said.

So I told him about the settlement, and what steps I had taken to protect my assets. "That's how I met Larry," I told Brad. "He's managing my money."

"You're rich," Brad gasped.

"Yes," I said. "I'm rich. But I don't want to use any of it except to make life a little easier. I want to move to a real apartment and buy a car. That's all I want for right now."

Brad got up and sat next to me again. "Do you realize that Carl has pissed away most of the settlement. Settlements for physical injuries are not taxable, or else he wouldn't even have enough left to pay the federal and state income taxes."

"How do you know that?" I asked in amazement.

"I've been taking courses on line for a few years now. I expect to get my bachelor's degree in accounting soon. I might even get to be a CPA someday. Being a regional director for Wendy's is great, but I want more."

"Do you think I could do something like that?" I asked. I am a high school graduate.

Brad gave me his beautiful smile. "Now that's something I can help you with. I'll help you get started on college courses on line. Wait, that's silly. You can afford to quit working and go back to school."

"No," I said. "I want to work. I need to work. I'll do it your way."

"Are we cool?" Brad asked.

"Yeah, we are ice cold," I answered him.

"Could we start all over? If we start from scratch, maybe I can win your heart," Brad said. I didn't want to comment on that statement.

"It's really late," I said. "I think you should spend the night." He undressed quickly and crawled into my small bed with me. He nested against me with his arm around me, and I was aware that his cock was limp. We fell asleep that way. Brad was comforting me, and neither of us had any thoughts of sex, at least not just then.

Brad left about 4 AM to go home, shower and get ready for work. When I arrived at work, we smiled at each other. I thought that Brad was the kindest guy in the world, but still, love seemed to elude me.

We had lunch together as was becoming our habit. At lunch I told him that Carl lived in his building, and that I would appreciate if he drove me there after work so I could find his car. When we got there, it wasn't hard to find Carl's car. There was an empty space next to it and Brad parked there. We both got out of Brad's car. I unlocked the Chevy and Brad and I got in.

I put the key in the ignition and turned it. The first time the car sputtered and didn't ignite, but on the second attempt the motor roared to attention.

"Let's test drive it," I said, and backed slowly out of the parking lot. The car was old, but it was all souped up. Obviously Carl had done a lot of work on it. I drove it around the neighborhood for awhile and then put it back in the parking lot.

"This car is great," I declared. "Brad can you give me a few hours off tomorrow? I can work the night shift if you want. I'd like to take the car to a mechanic and if it passes inspection, I'd like to get the registration changed to me."

"Sure thing," he said. "We'll manage without you for a few hours. I think that's a good idea. You said that you wanted to buy a car, and this one's an old fashioned beauty."

"I have another idea. It's not 5 PM yet. Do you think there's anyone in the rental office?"

"We can find out. What did you have in mind?"

"Maybe I can rent Carl's apartment. It's just like yours. He's one floor below you."

"Well, I don't think I can talk you into moving in with me so it would be great having you under me." He laughed at his double entendre.

As it turned out the manager of the complex was just getting ready to leave for the day, but he was glad to talk to a potential tenant. I told him that I was a friend of Carl Gilmore. Carl had informed me of his intention to move, and I wondered if I could rent his apartment.

"The manager thought the idea was good, but he seemed dubious about my ability to pay until Brad vouched for me.

"OK," the manager said. The rent is $900 a month. I'll require a security deposit of $900 and first and last month's rent. I'll prepare a one year lease. The movers are coming the day after tomorrow and I'll need a week to get the place ready. You can move in on December 20th if that's all right. You should be all settled by Christmas."

I shook his hand and agreed to come by at 4:30 PM the day after tomorrow to sign all the papers. My life was moving fast. Tomorrow I had to give my landlord notice as well as seeing to the car. I knew I would have to pay January's rent because of the one month notice rule, but it took me awhile to realize that it was merely pocket change.

When we left the manager's office, Brad threw his arms around me and said, "Welcome neighbor. This is going to be so great. We can car pool to work." He hesitated before going on. "I don't suppose you would like to spend the night with me?"

"Brad," I said. "You need to give me time to get over Carl. Let's compromise. Let's go to some good restaurant to celebrate my new apartment, but after that I'll drive myself home in my new used car."

Brad could do nothing but nod. It turned out that we had a great evening. Brad was aware that he wasn't going to get anything this evening, and I wasn't under any pressure to give anything, so we were both thoroughly relaxed and enjoyed each other's company. It seemed to me that it was easier being Brad's friend than falling in love with him. I remembered that some of the great love affairs throughout history started as friendships or feudships, and I wondered if our friendship could lead to love. Why couldn't I fall in love with Brad? Whatever the reason, it eluded me.

The first thing the next morning found me at a mechanic whom Brad had recommended. He was so thrilled with the car, he wanted to buy it. That was good enough for me. Then I went to the MVB with Carl's letter and the registration. I really lucked out here. The young clerk I finally got to see was obviously gay. He spotted me also, and was willing to accept Carl's letter to be a conveyance of the car to me as a gift. He transferred the title for a dollar to make it legal and gave me a new registration. When he handed me the registration, he included his card with it. I seriously thought of calling him, but a vision of Carl passed through my brain and I thrust his card in my pocket. I wondered if I would ever love again.

I drove my car to the bank and waited about a half hour, until I was able to see Larry. I told him about the car and the apartment. He was thrilled about my getting the car free and he had the bank transfer $2,700 from my money market account to my checking account so that I could pay for the rent and security deposit. Before I left, I told Larry that I would have him and Chuck for dinner as soon as I was settled.

"That reminds me," Larry said. "You're invited to our place for New Year's Eve. We are just having a few intimate friends over. You are always welcome to bring a friend."

"Right now I don't have anyone I'd care to spend New Year's Eve with other than you and Pop."

Disappointment covered Larry's face. "Please give that careful thought," he said as we kissed goodbye.

I thought about it for a long time. I reached into my pocket and carefully removed the card the guy at the MVB had given to me. I placed it in my wallet, and then I went to work. It was only 11 o'clock. I agreed with Brad that I would finish this shift and work the second. Right after Brad left, I called Gerald Thompson, the name on the card. When I reminded him who I was, he agreed immediately to go to the party with me. I made a date to go to his apartment the next evening after I gave my check to the rental agent at my new apartment.

The next evening, I went to the rental office and exchanged my check for copies of the lease agreement. From there I went to Gerry's apartment. He greeted me in his underwear, and in minutes we were in bed together. I enjoyed the sex with him but didn't care to stay the night. I made some excuse and took off. Before I left, I told him that I would pick him up at 9:00 PM on New Year's Eve.

"That's almost two weeks off," he reminded me. Won't I see you sooner?"

"Probably," I mumbled. "I'll call."

Everything I did after that caused Brad's face to register horrible pain, and I got a perverse thrill out of inflicting that pain. Was I crazy or what? Maybe I should see a shrink. After that, I turned down every invitation Brad offered me. When he asked me out for New Year's Eve I told him I had a date. The next day he called in sick. I exulted in the fact that I had made him sick. I was truly out of my mind.

The next morning at approximately 10 AM, everything began to spin around me. I lost the ability to stand up and I yelled Brad's name. He came running and he caught me, just before I collapsed.

- CHAPTER SIX -

I was in a coma for six days. I found out later that Larry, Chuck and Brad took turns holding vigil at my bedside. My 'adopted family' was not about to leave me alone. They spoke to me and held my hand. They bathed my forehead and kissed my lips. They showed me more love than I deserved and I was totally unaware of any of it.

I had suffered a brain aneurism. The doctors believed that it was probably caused by trauma resulting from the accident, but that couldn't be proved. I had signed off and relieved the cruise company of further liability anyway. I never should have signed the releases without an attorney, but I had relied on Carl. The hospital bills were sure to eat up all or most of my settlement.

The operation had been very delicate. The doctors were challenged to remove the sac and not cause any brain damage. Thank goodness for modern surgery. They were able to destroy the aneurism with laser beams. They drilled the tiniest of holes in my cranium, just enough to pass the laser through.

When I finally awoke, Larry was at my bedside. "Hi," he said.

"What happened?" I asked. I was frightened and I grabbed his hand.

"You'll be just fine," he said. "Chuck, Brad and I are taking care of everything." I didn't know what he meant, but I found out later. Brad had packed up my meager belongings at my apartment and moved them over to my new apartment. He arranged with the post office to forward my mail. Every few days, he started the motor on my car and let it run for awhile. When I had passed my sixth month anniversary at Wendy's as a full time employee, I became eligible for their health insurance. Brad made sure that all the papers were filled out and he submitted them for me. He did this when I was being so hateful to him. The insurance was effective the first of December before my collapse. At least eighty percent of the medical costs were covered. The remainder cleaned out my money market account.

Since I had been so cruel to Brad, he didn't think it was a good idea for me to stay with him during my recovery, so Chuck and Larry made arrangements for me to stay with them. They had a friend who was a nurse and he agreed to stay with me when they were at work.

When I was lucid enough to appreciate all the love they were showing me, I cried silently and thanked God for my new and caring family.

When I first woke up from the coma, Larry called the nurses. They asked me all kinds of silly questions, which I answered. With each correct answer, I could see the smiles on their faces. While they were interrogating me, Larry called Chuck and Brad who rushed right over. All three stayed with me until they saw that I was tiring. Chuck and Larry started to leave, but I asked Brad to stay behind. When we were alone, I asked him to kiss me. His feathery tongue sent shivers through my fragile body, just as it always did. Little by little, I remembered how badly I had treated him. Every time he came to visit me, I would beg for his forgiveness.

"The doctors told me that the aneurism was probably the cause of your strange behavior." Brad started to explain to me. "You acted like you hated me, but I never believed that. I just couldn't figure out why you were dismissing me from your life. I thought maybe it was because you didn't want to get involved in a relationship, in a committed relationship anyway. I had no idea that an aneurism was playing games with your brain."

"Can you forgive me?" I asked. "I am aware now that Carl is the biggest jerk in the world. I can't believe that I ever loved that loser."

In spite of our 'reconciliation' we went through with the plans for me to recuperate at Chuck and Larry, especially since Matt Crane, the male nurse, was willing to stay with me as a favor to my two dads. Matt told me later that he knew it would be for a short time anyway. He expected me to recuperate rapidly.

When I was released from the hospital, Matt helped me up the stairs to the guest bedroom at my dads' house. I was walking just fine, but a flight of stairs was a challenge. Larry and Chuck always left my door open at night so they could hear me should I need anything. Several times during my three week stay, I heard them making love. When they made love, I could clearly hear both of them repeating constantly, "I love you!" For some reason that always made me cry and I longed for Brad.

The day came for me to finally return to my new apartment. When Brad came to get me one Sunday morning, Chuck and Larry were crying. They hugged me like they didn't want to let me go. I had to remind them that we were coming on Tuesday evening for dinner, but they kept on crying anyway.

Matt came over also, with a bottle of champagne. "You and Brad can drink a toast to your new apartment," he said, as he handed me the bottle. "You're doing great," he said, and gave me a big hug.

When Brad and I entered the lobby of our building, the rental manager was there talking to a prospective tenant. He greeted me warmly and wanted to know why I had no hair. He was kidding of course. Brad had told him all about my surgery.

"It'll grow back," I promised him.

When I entered my apartment I was stunned. It was completely decorated, and I loved it. The décor was tasteful, classy and certainly not flamboyantly gay.

"How did you do this?" I asked.

"Hey man, I'm gay. Several of my friends are decorators and one of them did this for me. I had to tell him all about you so he could guess at your taste. I think he did a great job."

After viewing the entrance hall, living room and dining room, we went into the kitchen. The refrigerator was working as were the phones. Of course Brad had arranged for the utility accounts to be opened in my name. He thought of everything. We put the champagne that Matt had given me into the refrigerator, for later.

We went into the bedroom. The decorator had given me a king size bed. The minute I saw it, I got a momentary vision of making love in that bed, but I couldn't see who I was making love to. It did give me ideas, however.

I turned to Brad and began to kiss him. "Make love to me," I begged. "It's been so long."

"Are you well enough?" Brad asked. As usual he thought of my welfare before his.

"I think so," I answered. "If I feel that we shouldn't be doing something, I'll let you know. I don't need to be a hero."

"Ok," he said, "but I want you to just lie back and let me do all the work. I want to give you a welcome home present."

"But I want to make love to you too," I objected.

"There's plenty of time, love."

Brad was leaning between my legs and sucking passionately away at my cock. For the first time in my love making, whether it be Brad, Carl, Jorge or Gerry, I began to moan, "I love you, I love you Brad." As I said those words, my cum filled Brad's mouth and went down his throat. His mouth did not release my cock until it was limp, and I was begging for mercy.

We lay wrapped up together for quite awhile until Brad said to me. "Let's take a shower. Then I'll make dinner and we can have the champagne. I was so happy lying there in Brad's arms that what he said just wouldn't register. All I could reply to him was, "Please sleep with me tonight."

"I'd love to," he replied.

Brad would not let me return to work for another week. During that time, I called Brad's decorator friend to thank him for a job well done. "I guess you didn't get my bill yet," he joked. "All Brad does is talk about you. Nobody can be as perfect as he paints you. I can't wait to meet you. Brad asked me over for dinner Thursday evening so we'll be able to get acquainted.

"That's fantastic," I said. "See you then."

Brad and I had dinner at Dad and Pop on Tuesday, and they had all kinds of goodies for us. There were theater tickets, and gift certificates to fine restaurants and fine stores throughout the city.

"Why?" we asked.

"Because we love you," they answered. More tears.

On Thursday morning I received a bill from David Perkins, the decorator. He wasn't cheap, but I loved that he had done such a wonderful job and had saved me the trouble. I wrote a check to give him that evening.

Also in the mail were my first bank statements from the bank. I immediately reconciled my checking account. I had never done that before, but the reconciliation form was self explanatory and it worked out fine. The only outstanding check I had was David's.

I turned my attention to the money market account. After I paid the hospital and the doctors for the portion of the bill not covered by my insurance, all I had left from the original $50,000.00 was $5052.25. $2700.00 had gone for rent and the balance for medical bills. But according to the statement several deposits had been made during the month and the balance was now $6,750.25. I had asked Larry to deposit all interest and dividends to my checking account, but that was before he had decided on opening a money market account for ready cash. He must have changed the instructions. The additional money represented bond interest and dividends earned during the month. I was thrilled. I had added almost two months rent to this account in one short month.

Then I turned to a summary of my CD's. The $100,000.00 was now worth about $100,400.00 with the accrued interest. I was no genius, but I quickly figured out that I had earned approximately $2,100.00 in one month. If Brad wasn't making dinner tonight, I would have called him right up, and taken him to one of the fancy restaurants we had gift certificates to. Instead, I went outside and drove my car for the first time since my illness to a nearby bakery. I bought the most delicious, decadent dessert I could find. When I got home, I refrigerated the cake and then I called Brad.

"Brad Wilkinson," he said when he answered the phone.

"I love you," I said and hung right up. Then I waited for the phone to ring. Fifteen seconds later it rang. I was not disappointed except I had to wonder what took him so long.

"You fuck," he said. "You are simply impossible. How can you say you love me and then hang up on me?"

"Oh, didn't I tell you? I bought dessert for tonight."

"Good, I was going to stop and get something on the way home, but now I'll have time to fuck you before I start dinner."

"That sounds like a plan to me. Hurry your ass on home," I implored.

At about 4:00 PM, Brad came into the apartment. We had each other's keys. I was naked in bed waiting for him. He started stripping on his way to the bedroom and when he arrived all he had on were his socks. These were quickly discarded as he joined me in bed. We immediately wrapped our arms around each other and just cuddled.

"You feel so good," I said.

"So do you!"

Brad's hands began to wander all over my body. He didn't really linger anywhere, but he brushed by every spot he knew pleasured me. I had left condoms and lube on my bedside table and he put some lube on his finger. He inserted it into my ass and began to stretch me out. Then he lubed a second finger. This time he rubbed against my prostate and I began to moan.

"Now, do it now, please, now," I begged him. He threw me on my back and pulled me down so that my ass was at the edge of my bed. He lifted both my legs and placed his cock at my opening.

I pulled away. "You didn't put on a rubber," I said.

"At this point we shouldn't have to," he said. "I haven't been with anyone since the day you walked into my life."

"But I have. There was Carl, Jorge and I am ashamed to admit it, I had a one night stand just before my collapse. I always used protection, but you never know. Use a rubber now, but let's get tested as soon as possible. I don't want to ever have to use those things again. I am 100% committed to you, my love."

Reluctantly Brad put on the rubber, but it was worth it. When his cock went up my ass and massaged my prostate, I loved him so much, I could hardly bear the feelings I had for him. As he pumped me harder and harder the two of us kept yelling, "I love you!"

I insisted we shower together before Brad went upstairs to start preparing dinner. In the shower, Brad fell to his knees and went down on me. I was so euphoric in my love for him that I came after only a few strokes. That was just as well since Brad had a lot of work to do for tonight's dinner party.

We dried each other off and Brad just put on his trousers. He gathered up the rest of his clothes and took the back stairway up one flight to his apartment. As soon as I was fully dressed, I took the cake out of the refrigerator and used the elevator to go upstairs. Brad would be angry, but I intended to help him with his little dinner party.

I let myself in with my key and went right to the fridge with the cake. It was a battle to make room for it.

"Wait," Brad said. He removed a pork loin from the refrigerator. It was completely garnished and ready for baking. Brad put it on his counter and said, "The oven is pre heating. We'll pop this in when it's ready." Now I had room for the cake.

"I'll set the dining room table," I told Brad. When Brad saw that I was setting for three, he stopped me. "There will be six of us," he informed me.

"Who else is coming?"

"Well, David's partner George for one, and another couple."

Brad had been out for a long time, and had always lived in San Francisco. He had a lot of gay friends and I was anxious to meet them. I happily set up for six and asked what else I could do.

"Nothing," Brad said. "Just keep an eye on everything while I go dress."

"I'd rather keep an eye on you," I quipped.

"OK, peeping Tom, join me in the bedroom." As Brad dressed, I admired his rippling muscles, and hated when he covered them with his shirt. I got an erection when I saw him put on his pants without underwear. I thought that I would try that myself. It looked so sexy. When he was fully clothed, we hugged each other and kissed. If I live to be a thousand years old, I will never stop being thrilled by the way his tongue lightly flicks over mine. It simply sets me on fire.

I sat at the kitchen table while he basted the pork loin. Then he removed a covered dish from the fridge. It contained potatoes all peeled and ready for oven roasting. He deftly added them to the baking pan containing the pork loin. Then he took out two aluminum cans from his pantry. They both had green beans in them. He emptied them into a pot and put it on the stove on a low setting.

Then he went back into the fridge and removed a tray. The tray contained six individual servings of shrimp cocktail. He asked me to put one at each place setting, and he pulled another dish out of the fridge. He removed the saran wrap covering, and placed the dish in the middle of the table. It contained the cocktail sauce.

"I think I'm all set except for slicing the pork when it's ready," Brad said. Just then the doorbell rang.

Brad went to the door with me shadowing him. It was David and George. One of them was a flaming queen and the other was a macho man. I immediately assumed that the queen was David, my decorator. So much for stereotypes! Brad introduced me to them, and David was the macho one.

I took their drink orders and I was so familiar with Brad's apartment by now, I knew where everything was. I fixed them the drinks, and after I handed David his drink, I reached in my wallet and gave him his check.

"My God," he said, "you sure pay your bills quickly. I'll be glad to work for you anytime. By the way, you are as cute as Brad said you were," and right there in front of George he pinched my ass. Fortunately the door bell rang and I could get away without any awkward comments.

"I'll get it," I yelled to Brad as I was opening the door.

"Surprise!" I heard, and there stood Chuck and Larry. Their arms were full of packages.

"This is a surprise," I said. "What are all those packages?"

"Well, because of your little incident, you missed Christmas and the New Year's Eve party so we brought these along for a belated celebration."

"But I have nothing for you," I objected.

"Nonsense," Larry said. "You're alive. That's our gift."

I helped them put the packages on the hall table and then kissed them properly. I introduced them to David and George by their names, but then

I added, "Larry and Chuck are my dads." George's eyebrows went up at least an inch.

I knew that my dads would want wine, so I poured a glass of red wine for each of them. I was still on medications so I abstained, and Brad was too busy being a host to risk drinking any liquor.

"Do I have time to show Dad and Pop the great job David did on my apartment?" I asked Brad.

"I'll give you ten minutes."

My dads put their drinks on the coffee table, and went downstairs with me. They were as impressed as I had been with David's skills, and when we returned they were quick to compliment him.

David joked. "I love to be lauded, but here's my card in case you want to use my services." Larry put his card in his wallet.

Dinner was wonderful of course. I refilled George's drink twice more, but David refused saying that he was the designated driver. Larry and Chuck were satisfied with the one glass of wine.

Brad and I cleared the table. Then Brad said, "I'm putting up coffee and we have a delicious looking dessert. While the coffee is brewing let's open our Christmas gifts." He got the coffee going and then disappeared into his bedroom. When he came out, he had four packages. I knew immediately that he had gotten a gift for each dad from each of us. Is there nothing this man didn't think of?

Larry gave each of us a sweater and told us we should share. Chuck bought us each a dress shirt and a matching tie. He said we could share also. I knew that Brad and I were about the same size and build, but I had never thought of that in terms of sharing our clothing. That would certainly be a plus in our relationship.

Brad gave each dad a half dozen, calf high, dress socks for work. They were black of course. He also gave them two ties each, presumably from me. They were very conservative as befitted a banker and a professor.

I hated to see the party end, but eventually everyone went home. I stayed behind with Brad, and we didn't rest until everything was cleaned up and stored away. We placed the leftover food in plastic containers and froze them. Finally we collapsed on the couch.

I looked around and said, "You'd never know we had company."

"Sleep here with me tonight," Brad said.

"Was there ever a doubt?" I asked.

- CHAPTER SEVEN -

It was never a question of would we sleep together at night. The question was always in whose bed would we sleep? Little by little we began to discuss buying a house together.

Brad was adamant about everything being fifty-fifty. He said he could afford the down payment, but even though I could pay cash if I wanted to, he insisted on obtaining a mortgage. I said that I'd rather pay cash and he could pay me monthly for his half, but he wouldn't hear of it.

"Furthermore," he argued. "It makes no sense to deplete your principal as Carl has done, and mortgage interest and real estate taxes are good federal and state tax deductions."

Finally I realized that if we were going to commit to each other and live together, I had to do it Brad's way, that is to say, equally. At this point, I had been living in the apartment almost seven months. Coincidentally our leases expired a month apart so we figured we could move out in six months. We determined to close on a house in five months or less.

Larry and Chuck began to point out all the good points of buying in their neighborhood. The obvious was to be close to them. They also pointed out that a number of gay and lesbian couples lived in their neighborhood, and the area was very gay friendly. We checked out the part of the city where David and George lived, and areas where some of our other friends lived. In the end, we concluded that no place was too far away by car.

Larry and Chuck were family to us, and their neighborhood reminded us of the neighborhoods in the old family TV sitcoms, so we zeroed in on buying as close to Larry and Chuck as we could.

When we went looking at real estate we went in Brad's car. My car was souped up and a bit noisy. We didn't want any of the agents to think that we were disturbers of the peace.

My own peace was shattered, when I picked up my mail after work one day. I could see that one of the letters had been forwarded from my old address. I was surprised that it had been forwarded since I thought that the time limit had expired. The letter was from Carl, but the return address was different than the one he had given me. I ripped open the envelope and started to read:

Dear Aaron:

I tried to reach you by phone, but the number you gave me was no longer a working number. I suppose you have moved, but I am sending this letter to your old address hoping it will be forwarded to you.

I am returning to San Francisco. I called Burger King and they are taking me back as a store manager, but it may be in a different store.

I have been a complete fool. Gambling is legal at various Indian Casinos in Broward County, Florida. Jorge and I ran up heavy debts. Eventually I had to sell the condo and the Jaguar, and I depleted my settlement. We took a furnished apartment in a very seedy section of town and I got a job at a Burger King. Jorge went back to nursing.

We fought all the time, mostly about money. It seems that it was OK for me to support him, but he rebelled against the role of bread winner. I came home from work after the late shift one night, and Jorge was gone. He cleaned out the apartment. Not only did he take his stuff, he took most of mine too.

I decided to return home and to try to rebuild my life. Unfortunately my credit card has been cut off and I can't afford the air fare home. If you get this letter and if you could lend me $1,000 I'd be forever grateful. I promise to repay every penny. I would also appreciate if you could put me up until I find a place to stay. You are the only real friend I have in San Francisco. Please help me. My address is on the mailing envelope and my telephone number is 954-555-3344.

Your desperate friend,

Carl Gilmore

I put the letter back in the envelope and stuffed it into my pocket. My head was spinning and my mind was in turmoil. I was afraid of my emotions. As I read Carl's letter, my cock began to stiffen at the possibility of making love to him again. But I loved Brad, and we now had unprotected sex. If I ever cheated on Brad, I would have to use protection, not only with Carl, but with Brad too. How could I explain that? We were meeting Larry and Chuck for dinner tonight in The Castro. I would show them the letter and ask them what to do.

Larry and Chuck read the letter together and handed it to Brad. I could literally see Brad's face turn red as his blood began to boil, but he said nothing. Little by little he calmed down. When he felt that he was in control of himself, he said very quietly, "He almost ruined your life once. How can you entertain the idea of helping him unless you still love him?"

"Oh Brad, how can you think that? The only one I love is you." As I said those words, I couldn't help but wonder if it was true.

"You're being a little harsh, Brad," Larry said. "The boy's in trouble. He needs help and he has no one else to turn to"

"Let him try Traveler's Aid," Brad snapped back. "He made his own bed, and I don't want him dragging Aaron into it."

Was that a double entendre? I wasn't sure. One thing I was certain of. Brad was jealous, very jealous.

"What do you guys think I should do?" I asked, turning to Larry and Chuck.

There was silence for too long and finally Chuck answered. "If you give him the money because you want to help a fellow human being, a brother, in need, then I think you should do it. If you help him because you still have feelings for him, I don't think you should do anything without a joint decision by you and Brad. You committed yourself to Brad, Aaron, and that requires that you make a joint decision in either case."

"I don't trust him to pay Aaron back," Brad complained. "How do we know that he won't be constantly asking for money, and my good hearted partner will keep on feeding his sick needs?"

It was clear to me that Brad was harboring resentment along with jealousy. All I could say to him was, "That's not fair, Brad."

"I think I have the solution," Larry piped in. "Write him, or call him, and tell him that you have turned over all your settlement money to a financial manager. Tell him that the manager gives you a monthly allowance and pays all your bills. You have no authority to write checks unless the manager approves. I'll give you a bank check for $1,000 drawn on your account. I'll mail it to him with a promissory note that I will prepare. I'll ask him to sign and return the note. I'll enclose a return envelope addressed to me at the bank. The check will be restricted, and whoever cashes it must call me, your manager. The check will not be available until the manager gets his signed note and approves the check for payment."

"Wow," I said, "Can we do that?"

"Well, there is some truth stretching, but I believe that Carl would be made to realize that he has to pay you back, and that you can't be his money pit. Would you go for that, Brad?"

"Frankly Aaron, I don't think you should even answer his letter. I know that he was your first love, but he's just no good. Look how he has pissed away three quarters of a million dollars. He doesn't even mention in the letter if he is still in debt. What if he's leaving Ft. Lauderdale just to escape his creditors? Also I would object to you putting him up. I think you should tell him that you are in a committed relationship and your partner disapproves. That's the truth for sure."

I had never seen Brad act so unkindly, but I had to admit that if I was uncertain how I felt about Carl, Brad would certainly sense it, and want to keep me away from him.

"I could stay with you and he could use *his* apartment until he finds something."

I clearly heard Brad gasp and I corrected myself. "I mean *my* apartment." Brad jumped up and left the restaurant. I ran after him and found him leaning up against a street light at the corner.

"Brad, honey," I said to him. "I'll do whatever you ask me to do. I'll let Carl flounder if that's your wish, but I have never known you to be so dispassionate toward another human being."

"He's not another human being. He's Carl Gilmore. He has no ethics. He'll try to bleed you dry, and I'm afraid you'll let him. He dumped you once and he'll do it again. Now that he has reappeared in your life, I can tell that he has rekindled old feelings in you. You can deny it all you want, but I'm scared of him. I'm scared of losing you and I'm damn mad at you for even entertaining a thought of helping out that vulture."

"I haven't agreed to help him out yet. I haven't even called or written to him. Let's go finish dinner. We can talk more about it later."

When we got back, Brad was the first to speak. He looked straight at Larry. "I'm one hundred percent opposed to Aaron contacting this guy or lending him one penny, but I know he wants to do it. I think he still loves Carl even if he denies it. Let's do it your way, Dad."

Then he looked at me. "You can be a jerk and let him use your apartment, but I am telling you right now that I am going to fight for you. If I see him trying to win you over or trying to take money from you, I'll kill him. I'm not going to lose you, Aaron Jackson, especially not to a predator like Carl."

There was stunned silence. Finally Larry said to me. "Would you consider making my scenario come true?"

"What do you mean?" I asked.

"Well I would really manage all your money. I'd give you an adequate allowance and you would submit all your bills to me for payment. If there was something to pay that I didn't approve of, you would have to justify it to me. That way Brad wouldn't have to worry about Carl bleeding your money, and you would be telling Carl the gospel truth."

I was really stunned. I didn't like the idea at all. "What do you think Brad?" I asked.

"I could live with that," he answered.

"OK then, let's go for it."

"Be in my office late tomorrow afternoon to sign the papers. How much allowance do you want, son?"

"None," I answered. "I want to live on my salary."

"In that case," Larry said, "hand over your credit cards. I'll let you keep one for emergencies only. If I find that you abuse that card, I'll confiscate that one as well."

"I agree," I said. I could not read any emotion on Brad's face, and he was beginning to irk me. Conversation between the four of us was strained that evening and Brad and I didn't talk all the way home. When we got into the elevator, I hit the 2 button and Carl hit the 3 button.

The elevator opened at the second floor and I started to get out. Just as the doors began to close Brad darted out. He began to sob and scream at the same time.

"Please don't leave me alone. I don't want to lose you. I love you more than I love my own life. I don't demand that you love me as strongly. I only ask that you weigh your actions carefully in the light of possible consequences to our relationship. I need you in my life. I'll kill myself if you leave me." He couldn't say more because he was crying so badly.

For a moment I thought I had my aneurism back. I was totally fed up with Brad. He was smothering me. So what if I wanted to have Carl as a fuck buddy. It was none of his business. I vowed that I wasn't going to go along with letting Larry pay all my bills and giving me an allowance. I felt like my blood was boiling, literally.

However, I did not let my words or my actions betray my thoughts. I embraced him and said, "You're not losing me and stop being so foolish. Now come to bed with me and I'll show you how much I love you." The thing is I meant it. Carl, Carl, I thought, why do you have such a sexual effect on me? I don't need you. I have Brad. Shit! I still desire you.

The next afternoon, after my shift, I went to Larry's office. I decided to go through with his plans after all. I signed all the necessary papers. He prepared an envelope containing a letter of explanation to Carl, the promissory note and a bank check which indicated that the check was not valid unless approved for payment by the issuer. He also included a return envelope directly to his attention. The note required monthly payments of $50.00 and no interest. If he defaulted his salary could be garnisheed. Larry told me that it would be mailed tonight with the regular bank mail.

"This way," he said, "Carl still does not have your address or telephone number. He'll have to deal with me." I nodded in agreement.

"Now tell me," he asked. "Is everything cool with you and Brad?"

"He says it is, but I know he's totally opposed to my helping Carl out. Why is he being so foolish?"

"I don't think he's being foolish. Given your past relationship with Carl, I don't think you should have anything to do with him either. But it's obvious to me, Chuck and Brad that you have made up your mind to help him so at least we are taking steps to protect you."

A week later Larry called to tell me that Carl had returned the signed promissory note. There was a short note inside asking if I was going to let him shack up with me until he got his own place. Larry was quick to point out that nowhere in the note did he say thanks.

"I wrote him a note which I sent by overnight mail," Larry said. "I told him that he couldn't stay with you because you were in a committed relationship and your partner would not permit it. I told him that when he got here he was on his own. I told him that I didn't think he would have a problem finding a place since he had a good job. What I didn't tell him was your address or telephone number."

"Thanks Dad," I said and hung up.

I needed desperately to talk to him. I told Brad that I needed to take a break. Of course, the first thing Brad did was to worry about my well being. I was really getting tired of this puppy love.

I went into the alleyway behind the store and dialed the number Carl had given me. Someone with a thick Spanish accent answered the phone. I asked for Carl.

"He ain't here," the voice said and when I find him, I fix his sorry ass. You can tell him I say so." He hung up abruptly, leaving me upset and very worried. I waited until I was in my car going home and I called again. This time Carl answered. I did not mention my earlier call. I gave him my telephone number and told him to call when he got in and I would see what I could do about helping him find a place to stay.

Two days later Carl called me while I was eating dinner with Brad in my apartment. He gave me his flight number. He was arriving the next day late in the evening, and he wanted to know if I could pick him up. I said yes without thinking.

He would see that I was driving his old car. Technically he gave it to me, but he could ask for payment just the same, I suppose. Maybe I could call the loan an even exchange. Brad would kill me.

Then he would find out that I lived in his old apartment. How would he feel about that? Well, I was paying the rent, not him. I really should have called him back and told him that I couldn't help him, but I didn't do it. Instead I asked Brad if I could stay with him while Carl stayed at my place. Brad's reaction was violent.

"No, you fucking cannot. If you want him to stay at your place, you bloody well can stay with him. And you can cancel the meeting we have with that real estate agent on Sunday." He stormed out in the middle of our meal.

Without an aneurism, I was still hell bent on destroying my life. I tried calmly to understand what hold Carl had on me, but I couldn't. Instead I knew that I could get Carl into my bed tomorrow evening and I was hot for it to happen.

I began to worry about Brad. What should I do? Should I go upstairs, beg him to forgive me and tell him that I wouldn't pick up Carl after all, or should I take a fuck you attitude? I'll do whatever I damn well want to do. Who was Brad to forbid me from picking up Carl and giving him a place to stay? It's not that I didn't know that I was being self destructive, it's just that I wanted to hold Carl in my arms so badly that I didn't care.

At work the next day, Brad would not even say good morning. He only spoke to me if it was work related. A couple of times I caught him staring at me, but he looked away quickly. I wanted to grab him and tell him that I was all his, but I wanted Carl just as badly. Was it possible to love two guys at the same time? Maybe. I knew Carl wouldn't mind, but I wondered if Brad would go for a threesome. I didn't think so.

On the way home I stopped at a drug store and bought condoms and lubricant. There was no doubt in my mind that I would use them tonight.

I got to the airport way too early. I parked the car and went to the arrival gate. I could only go as far as the security gate so I found a seat and waited. I groaned when the board said that Carl's flight was a half hour late.

Somehow the time passed. I was standing beyond the gate scanning the faces of the arriving passengers. When I saw him I was shocked. I wasn't even sure it was Carl. He was a mere skeleton of his former self. He looked like he hadn't shaved in days and he desperately needed a haircut. I called his name, hoping he wouldn't respond and that it wasn't he.

When I called his name, he spotted me and smiled. With that smile, there was a semblance of the old Carl. He ran to me and threw his arms around me. He went to kiss me but his breath was foul. I pulled away quickly.

"All I have is this carry on," he said. "We don't have to go to baggage claim." I took him directly to my car. He climbed in without so much as a comment that I was driving his old wheels.

"We are making a few stops on the way home," I told him. Our first stop was a barber shop that catered to people who worked late. They opened at noon and closed at midnight. I got Carl a haircut and a shave and restored some of his former glory, but he still looked like a skeleton.

Then we went to a drug store where I bought him a razor, shaving cream, a toothbrush and some toothpaste. I pulled in to my apartment complex and was even more surprised that he didn't make mention of the fact that he used to live here. Worse yet, when we entered my apartment, he said, "Nice digs you have here, Aaron." Had he lost his memory or was he somehow mentally ill. Instead of questioning it, I merely said, "Thanks."

I showed him to the bathroom, and gave him a towel and wash cloth. "Why don't you brush your teeth and take a nice hot shower while I make us something to eat?" I asked him.

"I have nothing fresh to wear. All I own is what I have on."

I went to my dresser drawer, and found a pair of my gym shorts and no underwear. I had adopted Brad's habit of not wearing underwear. I handed the shorts to Carl and said, "You can wear this."

I heated up some linguini and meatballs that was left over from a couple of days ago. When Carl got out of the shower he was looking better and better. Unfortunately he still looked like a walking skeleton. His bare chest showed every rib.

"Where's your partner?" he asked. I thought I couldn't stay here. Your couch doesn't look too comfortable.

"He's away on business," I lied. "You can sleep in my bed with me."

"That's cool," he said and he sounded really enthusiastic. He ate the skimpy meal that I had prepared as if he hadn't eaten in days, and somehow I thought that might be the case.

I offered to make coffee, but he asked if I had the fixings of a gin and tonic. I mixed a drink for both of us. We settled down on the couch to enjoy our drink, and he said, "I must look like hell to you."

"Yes," I agreed. He smiled his special smile at me and I wanted him so badly. I moved closer to him just as the door opened. It was Brad. I forgot that he had my key.

He looked daggers at Carl and said to me. "I'm really sorry, Aaron. I said that I would fight for you, and I intend to. I love you too much to let you get away from me. Please, come stay with me and let Carl stay here."

"Who the fuck are you?" Carl said. He jumped up and put his face in Brad's.

"Carl, sit down," I ordered. "This is Brad, my partner. I lied to you when I said he was away on business."

Brad gave a little sigh that sounded like a sob. "Please come upstairs. If you want me to, I'll beg. Forgive me for the way I acted. It's just that I was so jealous. Don't throw away what we have."

I knew I should take Brad's hand and leave with him, but two things stopped me. First, I didn't want him to win this battle and second, I really wanted to have sex with Carl.

"Brad," I said, "I love you. I truly do, but I want to have sex with Carl tonight. Would you consider joining us?"

Brad looked stunned. I could tell that he wanted to lash out and run out of the room, but he remained calm. After all, he said that he was fighting for me.

"It's not what I do," he whispered. I barely heard him.

"But it's what I want. If you truly love me, you'll honor my wish.

- CHAPTER EIGHT -

"Stop it! You're both acting like fools," Carl yelled at Brad and me. "Who the fuck says I want to sleep with either one of you? Aaron you are acting like a simpering love sick teen ager, which you are by the way. And you Brad, you're acting like sex was some kind of sacred cow. Sex is for fun; love is a commitment. A commitment doesn't mean you can't stop having fun."

Brad and I were speechless. Instinctively he took my hand. It was an unconscious act to try to protect me from the hurt he knew that I must be feeling. Carl sat down on a chair and he buried his head in his hands.

"I'm impotent," I thought I heard him say.

"What?" Brad asked.

"I'm impotent," Carl said louder. He looked up at me and reached his hand out. I took it in mine.

"I lied to you," he said. "I didn't lose everything because of gambling. It was drugs. Jorge knew a dealer and we got high just about every night. At first sex was glorious in that condition. The high was just that, a high! My orgasms were so heightened I could barely stand it. But as we fell deeper and deeper into the abyss, neither of us could even get an erection. The only thing that rose up was our debts.

"One night, in some seedy boarding house where we rented a room, we both overdosed. The owner of the house didn't find us for about eighteen hours. Jorge was dead and I was rushed to the hospital." He stopped and looked at me.

"Ironically it was the same hospital where we recuperated from the accident. I wasn't there very long. They couldn't do much for me, and they wanted me to go to a rehab. I had no money and no insurance. I was diagnosed as being HIV positive and a drug addict, so they arranged to send me to some state run facility. It was the pits, but at least they got me sober. The only way I can stay that way, is to keep on taking the drugs they prescribed for me, but the meds continue to leave me impotent. I'll have to be on those drugs forever. Who knows if I'll ever have sex again, protected sex or not."

He was silent and then he started sobbing. His chest began to heave and he could hardly breathe. None of us could say anything. I got him a glass of water, and he drank it slowly.

"I'm sorry," he said to both of us. "Please just let me stay the night and I'll find a place tomorrow, I promise. I still have about $350 of the $1,000 you gave me, Aaron, so I can make a security deposit."

"Brad said, "Why don't you stay until you have a couple of pay checks under your belt. You don't need to strap yourself. I have a feeling that Aaron is finally ready to move in with me. If you stay we can keep an eye on you and make sure you're fit to start work. When do you start by the way?"

"I'll go to the office tomorrow and get things rolling. I feel better already."

"We go to work very early," I said. "I'm just going to take work clothes for tomorrow and we'll see you when we get home. You can use my car to get to the Burger King office. The keys to the apartment and the car are on the front hall table. We get home about 4:30 so try to be here by then so you can fill us in on the events of the day.

I went into the bedroom, and took some fresh clothes for the next day. I already kept a supply of toiletries in Brad's apartment, as he did in mine. We both gave Carl a hug and left him.

The elevator was too slow for us and we bounded up the stairs. When we got to Brad's apartment, I hugged him as hard as I could. "I've been an idiot," I said.

"I know." he said, "but I love you too much to care right now."

"Fuck me, fuck me senseless," I implored Brad. I need you inside of me so I know that we are truly one body."

Brad kissed me in the special way that melted my soul and eliminated any inhibitions that might reside in me. "My pleasure," he purred in my ear.

That night as we made love, I no longer yearned for Carl. I didn't even think of him once. All uncertainty had abandoned me, and I knew that Brad and I were bonded forever. I didn't need drugs to achieve an orgasm that left me screaming from the joy of it. After we made love we fell into a peaceful sleep wrapped up in each other's arms. When the alarm went off at 4:30 AM, we were still in that position.

We stayed like that until the last possible moment. Then we did our morning necessities and showered together. It was also tough getting out of the shower. We didn't need to consider breakfast. We could always have breakfast at work.

During the day, we were oblivious to customers and staff. Every time we brushed by each other, we kissed. I think my jaw was fixed in a permanent grin. At lunch time we both ran over to the bank and asked one of the customer service reps to please interrupt Larry, who was with a client. It was really important and we needed his time for just a moment. As quickly as we could we told him about last night.

"Come over to the house this evening," he said. "I want to hear all the gory details. I love you both, my sons," he said with a slight sob in his throat.

As an afterthought, he added. "Don't bring Carl. I want us all to be able to talk freely. We'll meet him another time."

I noticed that whether Chuck was around or not, Larry always spoke in the plural. He had just said, "We'll meet him another time." I would have expected him to say "I'll meet him another time." Larry and Chuck were truly coupled. They always thought of each other in the plural. I hadn't achieved that with Brad yet, but at that second I knew it would happen.

When we got home, we went straight to my apartment. I knocked on the door and was not happy that there was no answer. Brad let us in with his key. He entered the apartment first and I heard him gasp. "Oh my God," he yelled.

I walked in behind him and cried out in pain. The apartment was in shambles. Every drawer in the kitchen had been turned inside out and the contents were on the floor. We went into the bedroom, and I flew to the top drawer in my dresser. I always kept about fifty dollars of mad money there and it was gone. My closet and my dresser drawers were cleaned out. Most everything I owned was gone. I ran to my bedroom window. I was able to see the parking lot and my car from there. Of course, the car was gone too. Also gone were several beautiful living room accessories that David had purchased for me. I figured that the only reason he would take more than clothes was for drug money. I sat down on my bed and started to cry.

Thank God Brad took charge. He called the police and my insurance company. He also called a locksmith's emergency number. Then he called Larry and Chuck and told them what had happened and cancelled our date. They said that they would be right over.

The locksmith was actually the first to arrive. He changed the locks and gave me two keys. I gave one to Brad and asked him to please make a duplicate for the management office.

The police arrived as the locksmith was finishing up. They were in the apartment for a long time taking my statement, and pictures of the appearance of the apartment. They looked for fingerprints even though we were able to identify the perp. Before they arrived, Brad had already taken pictures for the insurance company. He especially took pictures of the empty closets and empty drawers. He assured me that David could get invoices to prove the value of the missing accessories.

Larry and Chuck arrived just as the police were leaving. The sweethearts had brought us dinner. I didn't think I could eat anything but once I tasted the food, I ate it all.

To his credit, Brad never said 'I told you so.' But I said, "Brad honey, you were so right. I should never have answered his letter. What a fool I am."

Brad put his arms around me and pushed my head down on his shoulder. "Well, don't take this wrong," he said. "I'm kind of glad this happened. Now you can get him out of your system and love me as fully as I love you."

"Here, here," I heard Chuck say.

"I got him out of my system last night," I said to Brad. "Couldn't you tell that when you were fucking me?"

"TMI boys," Larry warned us and started laughing.

We all went about replacing all the kitchen stuff that Carl had thrown on the floor. When the kitchen was looking normal we straightened out the other rooms. That was easier. The living room had gaps where the stolen accessories had been and the bedroom looked normal until you opened the closets and drawers.

Brad helped me change the linen on the bed. I didn't know if Carl had slept on my bed at all, but I didn't want to risk sleeping on sheets that he had slept on.

When they saw that there was nothing more that they could do, Chuck and Larry took their empty dishes with them and went home. Brad said that he would stay with me. We didn't want to leave the apartment in case the police had something to report to us.

They did. At about 11 PM, the detective who had taken my statement called. He told me a hair raising story.

At about 9:30 PM a highway patrolman spotted the stolen car coming off the Oakland Bay Bridge. He put his flashers on, but the car didn't stop. Instead the driver increased his speed. He was driving way too fast and very erratically. At one point, he had reached a speed of 110 mph. He lost control of the car at an over pass. He hit the railing and flipped over. The car fell 25 feet onto the road below and burst into flames. It was a miracle that he didn't hit another car, and that all the other cars on the road were able to avoid the conflagration. The detective noted that it was fortunate that it was way past rush hour.

The driver was killed outright, the car was totaled and the contents of the car were destroyed. It was almost impossible to tell if my belongings had been fenced prior to the accident or not. At any rate, nothing could be salvaged. An autopsy was being performed to determine if alcohol or drugs was a factor. "Confidentially," the detective said, "he was so badly burned, I don't think that they will be able to determine anything."

"How ironic," I said to Brad. "He survived the bus accident only to end up like this. The money he received in settlement directly led to his death. What a waste."

Brad said, "Thank God you were wiser and more mature about how to handle the settlement money."

I thought I should be having some feelings about the death of someone I thought I loved, but strangely, I didn't feel anything. I was emotionless. I felt nothing at all until Brad put his arms around me, and then I felt comforted, safe and protected.

The next day, Brad insisted that I take the day off to start replacing my stolen goods and to get my insurance claims going. I may have had money in the bank, but I was still in the habit of being frugal. I went to a nearby Chevrolet dealership and purchased a late model, low mileage used car. It was fuel efficient and serviceable. I had to call Larry to help me figure out how I was to pay for this.

When he arrived at the dealer, he told me that he took the rest of the day off to help me get back to some sort of normalcy. He handled the finances with the car salesman while I called the insurance company to get the car insured and to remove the demolished car from the policy. I told the insurance agent that I was coming over to fill out the claim forms. They had already started a numbered file based on Brad's call from the day before.

The dealership said I could pick up the car in three or four hours. They wanted to spiff it up for me.

Then Larry and I went to JC Penney where I always bought my clothes. The salesman must have been glad to see me because I had to buy everything from socks and shoes to shirts, ties and jackets. Larry took particular delight in choosing the sexiest underwear for me, which he insisted was his treat. I whispered in his ear that neither Brad nor I wore underwear. "You will need them for special occasions," he said. I decided not to argue.

Next stop was the police station, where I was given a copy of the burglary report. The investigating detective gave me the report and told me that the corpse was too damaged to autopsy, just as he had suspected. My stomach began to churn and I got out of there quickly.

We had a quick lunch in a coffee shop, and then we went to the insurance company. My agent read the police report and made a copy for his files. The report not only contained the details of the burglary, but the detail of the accident as well. I told him I could get him pictures if he needed them and invoices for the expensive accessories..

"Don't bother," he said. "The maximum claim for lost contents on your renter's insurance is $1,000, so that's all you'll get. It won't be a problem. Your loss was obviously greater than that. As for the car, you'll get blue book value. Even though lots of work had been done on it, we can't reimburse you for that.

On the way out of the insurance office I said to Larry, "Between the uncollectible promissory note, the lost contents of my apartment, and the automobile, Carl managed to cost me plenty of bucks in spite of your best efforts to protect me.

We both laughed ironically. "By the way, son," Larry said. "You're a big boy and a frugal one. Let's go back to our old arrangement. This arrangement is too complicated. I just have to move some money around to minimize your loss, and then we'll go back to normal."

Larry drove me back to the car dealer, and he left me with a kiss. He went home and I went back to Wendy's to wait for Brad. I decided that I wanted to take him out for a celebration dinner. I still had my credit card.

About two weeks later we went to contract on the house of our dreams. We must have seen a zillion houses and I could tell that our agent was getting a wee bit annoyed with us. Too bad! This was a big move for us and we didn't want to settle. Larry had helped us get pre-approved for a mortgage which was greater than we would actually need, so neither we nor the seller had to worry about not being approved.

The house was situated on a corner lot on our dads' street. Our back yard abutted the back yard of a lesbian couple and the house next to us was owned by a gay couple. They were the same age as Chuck and Larry, and they in turn, were separated by two houses. All of this was a selling point, especially when we found out that these couples were good friends of our dads and we would have met them last New Year's Eve had I not so inconveniently collapsed. In fact, the evening we went to contract we were invited to our dads' house, along with Nurse Matt, for dinner. After dinner our new neighbors came in to meet us, and to wish us many years of good health in our new home. Larry and Chuck kept hugging us. They were the two happiest people I had seen in ages, not counting Brad and me of course.

The seller gave us permission to come over with David. We wanted him to help us decorate. He liked what he saw and made copious notes. We had him and George over for dinner a few nights later. After dinner, he toured both of our apartments and suggested what we should take to the new house and what we could sell or give to charity. For sure that was going to make our move a lot easier.

We spent our days off packing, meticulously marking each box as to contents, and what room the box should be put it in. When we took a break we made love to each other. Now that there were no barriers between us, we could not get enough of each other. Strangely, achieving orgasm seemed less important than just touching, caressing, fondling and plain old fashioned cuddling. That's true love.

On the evening before the move, we slept in Brad's bed. We still had my bedroom set. It was slated for bedroom two in the new house. Before going to bed we showered together, making sure that our bodies were nearly antiseptic. Now we were ready to celebrate our last night together before our final commitment to live together.

Our kisses were long and sensuous. Every time I tried to move down Brad's body, he tried to do the same to me and we were making no progress. Finally we had to agree to play sixty-nine. It was not our favorite thing to do, because we both found it distracting. However, this night we were both so aroused that it turned out to be wonderful. I was sucking Brad's cock which I always loved to do, and he was returning the favor.

My orgasm was coming before Brad's and I was too excited to keep on sucking him. I had to stop until he brought me to orgasm. When I calmed down slightly I took him back into me, concentrating only on his pleasure. We both swallowed every bit of our cum, and then hugged so tightly nothing could have come between us. It was a marvelous way to fall asleep.

We were up early to greet the movers. We had been packing for weeks and had brought everything to the new house ourselves. All the movers had to do was to move the big pieces of furniture. By noon of moving day, all the furniture they had brought was set up properly in the new house. Previously, we had unpacked and gotten rid of all the boxes that we had moved over to the new house by ourselves. The contents of the boxes were all stowed where they should be, including all our clothes.

Brad took my hand and walked us into the master bedroom.

"Behold OUR bedroom," he said. Then he leaned into me and kissed me, taking my breath away.

"Welcome to our new life," he said.

- CHAPTER NINE -

Late the following May, Brad received his bachelor's degree in accounting. The on-line school transferred all his credentials to UCSF and he actually went through all the ceremonies of the graduating class right along with them. Our dads and I must have taken a thousand pictures of the event.

Several CPA firms advertised in a few of the local gay publications. We and our dads spent some time discussing the pros and cons of trying to get employment with a gay owned firm as opposed to one whose politics might be questionable. Brad thought that he could do well in a standard firm, but if there was a hint of homophobia it could hinder his career. We all agreed, but felt that in the end, it would probably not make a difference. Brad decided to try the firms which advertised in the gay press first, and see what would happen.

He sent his résumé to five firms. At Larry's suggestion, he enclosed one of his graduation pictures. Four of them called and set up interviews. The fifth said that they had no openings at present, but would be happy to keep his résumé on file.

Brad went to all four interviews. Two firms called back and said that they were sorry but the job had gone to another applicant. The other two offered him employment as a junior accountant. There was a slight difference in the salary offered, but not enough to influence Brad's decision.

"Here's the thing," he said. "Firm one is well established. The partners are about our dads' ages. I can learn a lot from them. Firm two is owned by two young men, not much older than I am. They're life partners also. They have been in practice for less than four years, but they are expanding like crazy. They said that even hiring me might not be enough. If they are still overwhelmed when I start work, they would hire yet another man. I would be coming in on the ground floor of a growing practice, and I feel more comfortable with them because we are contemporaries."

"It sounds like you have made up your mind to go to firm two," I said.

"Yes, I think so, but I want to hear your opinion."

"You're young," I said. "You have room for a few decision making mistakes. Go for the growth company." I started to laugh.

"What's so funny?" Brad asked.

That's what Larry would say, "Go for the growth company."

"Well," Brad said, "Larry never steered us wrong yet."

In the morning Brad called firm two, Pickler and Underwood, and accepted their job offer. They agreed that he would start in two weeks on a Monday morning and admired his integrity for wanting to give two weeks notice at his present job. James Pickler asked if he was free for dinner that night. He and his partner, Jim, ("Call me Jamie to avoid confusion.") would like to take him and his partner out to dinner. Brad accepted for us and we agreed to meet at our favorite gay owned restaurant at 7 PM.

"They're clients of ours," Jamie said. "I'm pretty sure they will give you the same discount in the future as we have. I'll introduce you to the owner tonight. I'm looking forward to meeting Aaron," he said as he hung up.

Brad took a moment to hug me before calling firm one and telling them that he had decided on a different firm. They expressed their disappointment and graciously wished him good luck. Then he called our dads who wanted to take us to dinner to celebrate, but when he told them that we were invited to dinner by the bosses, they took a rain check.

"Where are you going?" Larry asked.

"To Alfredo's, on Market Street." Brad answered.

There was only one thing left to do. Brad went to his computer and typed up a letter of resignation. What I didn't know at that time is that he recommended me as his replacement.

We got to Alfredo's a few minutes early but Brad spotted Jamie and Jim at the bar. He went over and extended his hand, but they both stood up and embraced him warmly. Brad was right. They were about twenty-eight years old, and exceptionally handsome. I knew why they were expanding so rapidly.

Brad introduced me to his new bosses, and Jim said, "If I had a boyfriend, this young and this good looking, I'd keep him locked up." I blushed a deep red.

The waiter showed us to our table and Jamie insisted that we order a cocktail. Neither of us drank much and I got out of it by saying that I was on medications. That was no lie. The doctor still had me on blood thinners, but he promised to stop them soon. Brad ordered a gin and tonic and as he was sipping it, he kept adding ice from his water glass to cut it down.

The waiter was just clearing away our appetizers, and cleaning the table with a little brush in preparation to serving our entrees, when I heard a familiar voice yell, "Jamie, Jim, imagine meeting you here."

I looked up to see Dad and Pop. They were ignoring Brad and me, but Larry was shaking our hosts' hands and saying how nice it was to run into each other like this. He took a moment to introduce Jamie and Jim to Chuck. They shook his hand warmly.

"It's about time we met," Jamie said to Chuck.

"Yes," Jim echoed. He turned to us and said, "Let me introduce you guys. This is Larry Reilly. He's our banker, and this is his partner Chuck Harrington.

To tell the truth, Brad and I didn't know what to say. We also didn't know what to do. Should we pretend to be strangers and shake hands or tell the truth?

The decision was taken out of our hands. Chuck bent down and kissed Brad on his lips and Larry did the same to me, and then they switched.

"No introductions are necessary," Larry said. "You are having dinner with our two sons."

"Well, I'll be damned," Jim said.

Brad was a little upset. "Did you guys know about this before, and did it influence you in hiring me?"

"Believe me," Jamie said. "This is as much a surprise to us as it is to you. You were hired because we think you are the right man for the job. Your track record of hard work, dedication to your employers and your managerial skills are what we looked at. The fact that Larry and Chuck consider you to be their sons is a very pleasant surprise, and just proves that we made a wise choice."

Jim asked Chuck and Larry to join us, but they declined. "We four, or at least we three, know each other well. Please get to know my sons. I think you will be pleased at what you learn about them." They went to the waiter who seated them at a separate table.

Jamie and Jim kept the conversation away from business, maybe because of me. We learned that they had met in college and in their sophomore year they took a room together off campus. Unlike my terrible story, both had come out to their parents in high school and each set of parents had fallen in love with their son's partner. They were fortunate enough to enjoy a great relationship with their parents and siblings.

I told of my excommunication and of not having seen my parents or my two sisters since they threw me out. They all expressed sympathy and I said, "There is no sympathy needed here, I have my two dads, who are better parents than my real parents ever were. Most of all I have Brad, who makes my life a Garden of Eden." Brad laid his hand on mine.

"How about you Brad?" Jamie asked.

"There's not much to tell," he said. He must have been right. I was suddenly thunderstruck. Brad had never talked about his life before I met him, and stupidly I had never asked. My life was so full of drama, that I had neglected the one I loved most dearly in the world.

"Please Brad," I said, "I want to hear."

"My father was an alcoholic. He deserted us when I was four years old. My mom was vague about it, but I gather he got into a drunken brawl one night and almost killed someone. He ran off to escape the police and we never saw him again." I grabbed Brad's hand, but he continued.

"My mother could not care for me so about a year later, she put me into the foster care system until she could get on her feet. Every day I looked for her to come and get me, but she never did, and in a short time, I could not remember either one of my parents. To this day, I don't know what became of either of them.

"The first few years were the toughest. I had a series of foster parents who were no better than my father. I was constantly abused and one of them beat me repeatedly when I was about eight." I squeezed Brad's hand.

"Finally I ran away, and when the authorities found me, they put me in another home. Most of the places they sent me to weren't bad, but I never seemed to be in any one of them long enough to bond with any of the parents. Yet with Chuck and Larry I bonded swiftly.

"When I was eighteen, I left the system and got a job at Wendy's. I started working on my bachelor's degree on line and you guys know the rest."

We were all silent until finally Jim said. "That's the past Brad, and Jamie and I promise you a brighter future." He raised his glass and we drank to that. It was water for me.

At the end of the meal we sat and chatted for awhile. Then our dads came over and asked if we would join them in an after dinner drink.

"Yes, please," Jamie said, and we made room for two extra chairs.

Jim said, "This evening has been a totally unexpected pleasure. Chuck, Larry never stops telling us what a great guy you are and we actually got to meet you tonight. I was beginning to think you were a figment of Larry's imagination. Then the perfect candidate walks into our office for an interview, and he turns out to be our banker's son. A little nepotism never hurt any business."

"I'd like to propose a toast," Larry said raising his glass. "Here's to the continued success of Pickler and Underwood, and here's a wish for continued good health, and good fellowship for all of us." We all clicked our glasses (mine was still water) and drank to the sentiments of the toast.

We chatted a little while and then Chuck and Larry got up to leave. "Goodnight," Larry said, "to my favorite sons and my favorite clients." We all stood up and of course Chuck and Larry kissed Brad and me on the lips, but in contrast to the formal handshakes at the beginning of the evening, they embraced Jamie and Jim and kissed them on the lips also. Their kisses were returned.

Finally Brad said, "This is great fellas, but tomorrow is a working day and Aaron and I get up at 4:30 AM so we'll have to call it a night. We can't thank you enough for this great dinner."

Pickler and Underwood both groaned when Brad said 4:30 AM. "Well, you'll be able to sleep a lot later than that in a couple of weeks, unless you are a light sleeper, and Aaron wakes you two hours before dawn," Jim said.

Everyone laughed at that, and we all stood up to leave. We were all a little awkward not knowing exactly how to part, until Jamie said, "Look guys, let's have no formalities here. We're friends." With that he embraced Brad and kissed him on the cheek. I guess he felt that lip kissing could come later. He kissed me also, and then Jim repeated the process.

We didn't get home until 11 PM and we knew that we wouldn't get much sleep that night, so we reluctantly gave up sex, but we fell asleep wrapped up in each other's arms with our cocks grinding together.

At 9 AM the next morning, Brad left me in charge of the store and drove to the regional office to deliver his resignation letter personally. There were more expressions of disappointment, but in the end they wished him good luck.

At about 11 AM the next day, one of the executives from our regional office came in and took Brad into the small office in the rear. After about five minutes, Brad called me in. He introduced me to Mr. Stigler, who shook my hand warmly. Then Brad said, "Aaron, Mr. Stigler is your new boss. On my recommendation he's promoting you to store manager. You'll be getting a substantial raise and I can't think of anyone more deserving, even if you are my partner." He said that right in front of Mr. Stigler. I had to admire Brad for his openness about being gay. I was still very reserved about saying anything to indicate that I was gay.

Mr. Stigler shook my hand warmly and said, "Brad will show you the ropes and break you in. Your promotion is effective the day Brad leaves." He opened up his briefcase and took out a sheet of paper.

"Why don't you guys post this on the bulletin board?" He handed the paper to me and I saw that it was a memo to the staff informing them of my promotion. I was suddenly so proud of myself and of Brad also. I could almost picture this event a few years down the pike, when I handed over the reins to some deserving young person. Brad had started me on my on-line college career. I was majoring in education with a minor in math. My goal was to teach math at the high school level. I was nearly finished with my first two classes. Brad made sure that we never let our private lives interfere with my studies, and he kept my nose to the grindstone. I knew well enough how his education was beginning to pay off for him, and I couldn't have had a better role model.

As Mr. Stigler left, I thanked him profusely. As soon as he was out the door, the staff that was present surrounded me and to a man they all wished me the best of luck. There wasn't too much for Brad to show me. I had been assisting him for weeks. I knew how to prepare all the daily, weekly and monthly reports. The only thing I hadn't done was accompany him to the regional office to see who got what report. From then on, I followed him like his shadow, which wasn't a stretch for me at all.

The next two weeks went really fast, and I was glad for Brad's sake. He was so anxious to begin work at Pickler and Underwood, CPA's, PA, that he could hardly sleep. The abused little foster care boy had come a long away and his future was really looking bright. By the time he left I was comfortable with my new job, but sad to realize that Brad and I would be separated all day every working day. Well, such is life and we would get used to it.

For his part, Brad was really starting at the bottom rung of the ladder. On the very first morning, Jim took him to a client and started him on the first job every budding CPA begins with, the dreaded bank reconciliations. With that done, things got more interesting. Jim showed Brad how to verify accounts receivable by checking the receipts subsequent to the audit date. Similarly with accounts payable, Brad checked the cash payments subsequent to the audit date, and actually found a duplicate payment. He brought it to Jim's attention, who then informed the owner of the business, who thanked both men. "The guy I double paid would never have informed me or credited me with the extra payment," he said. "Rest assured."

Each day, Brad came home more excited at all he was learning. He was particularly grateful for the patience shown by Jim and Jamie. One evening, he came home particularly excited. He, I, Chuck and Larry were invited to a barbeque at Jim and Jamie the following Sunday afternoon. They had also invited a few of their gay clients.

As if that wasn't enough, Jim had told Brad that they had a brand new client. He was small and just starting out but he had great potential. He was opening a small boutique, and Brad was going to handle the account solo.

I was so excited for him, that I made him turn in early. It was one of those nights where I wanted to do all of the love making and let him just lie back and enjoy himself. I don't think my tongue missed a square inch of his body, front and back. Certain orifices received particular attention.

I teased him unmercifully until I zeroed in on his balls and cock. I almost brought him to orgasm several times but always stopped before the point of no return. Finally, I stopped to lubricate his cock and my ass. I squatted over him and gently lowered myself on to his cock, which was jerking in its desire for attention. When I had him all the way up my ass, we began a dance of love until he exploded inside of me. I sat still on him until his limp dick fell out. Then I scooted down and ate my cum which was dripping from his luscious ass.

He desperately wanted to return the favor but I told him that he was to just go to sleep. Tonight was my treat. We lay together as close as we could get and I felt his hand fondling my cock. I wanted to tell him to stop, but it felt too good and I eventually came in his hand. We fell asleep, too tired to change the sheets.

The barbeque at Jim and Jamie was spectacular. They actually barbequed filet mignon steaks. I must admit a weakness for filet mignon. They served this with corn on the cob which they barbequed in tin foil. There was plenty of soda and beer. I was off the blood thinners and I enjoyed a couple of beers. As you can see my Mormon days were far behind me.

Besides us and our dads there were two other couples, all clients of the firm. One of the couples was the owner of Alfredo's. Brad already knew all four of them, and he introduced them to me, Larry and Chuck.

I was making small talk with one of the couples when I suddenly felt a hand squeezing my ass. I panicked for a moment and then decided to ignore it. As soon as I could, I excused myself and left. Immediately I told Brad what happened, and he started to laugh. "They're harmless," he said. "They do that to me all the time. They are totally devoted to each other, but flirt all the time." That did make me feel much better. By the end of the barbeque we were making arrangements to socialize with the other two couples, and with Jamie and Jim, of course. I was so happy that I sensed it could not last.

On the morning after the barbeque, I was in my office working on a report, when one of my staff knocked on the door.

"There's a guy out there says he's a friend of yours and would like to see you for a moment."

Did he give a name?" I asked.

"I'm afraid not."

I walked out to the store and there standing to the side of the serving counter was Carl Gilmore. I had to grab something to keep from falling. It was not the scrubby Carl I had last seen, but a healthy looking young man. He looked like the Carl I knew from the hospital bed.

"Can we talk privately for a minute?" he asked, and I led him into my office and closed the door.

- Chapter Ten -

The moment the door was closed, Carl leaned into me in an attempt to kiss me, but I turned my face. He managed to brush my cheek.

"Talk," I said, "before I go crazy. You're supposed to be dead."

"I know," he said. "When I read in the paper that the body in the wreck was identified as me, I decided to leave it that way. I owe a fortune of money in Florida and California. I figured that if I stayed dead, I could create a new identity, and rebuild my life." He started to cry. "You know I'm not a bad person," he said. "It was the drugs."

"But who the hell was in the car with all my stuff?" I demanded to know.

"After you and Brad went to work, I searched your apartment for drug money. I found $50 in a drawer and I called a dealer I knew. I lied when I said I was clean."

"I knew it. You didn't look clean to me," I interjected.

"I'm afraid I wasn't too neat searching for money. I made a mess and I am sorry for that. When the dealer arrived, he took the money and reached into his pocket. I thought he was reaching for drugs, but he pulled out a gun and pistol whipped me. I passed out, and when I came to, the apartment was a bigger mess than I had left it. I looked around and saw that he had taken all your clothes and some of the contents of your home.

"I ran to get the car keys to get away. I wanted to run as far away from you as I could because I was so ashamed. Of course, the car keys were gone. I snatched the house keys, locked up and just started running. I had no idea where I was going. The body in the car must have been the dealer."

"Where did you go? What did you do?" I asked.

I stayed at a homeless shelter where I had no access to drugs, and I got clean and sober with a great deal of pain and effort. The people at the shelter gave me some clean clothes and I got a job in a greasy spoon waiting on tables. It was a beginning. I'm working for a good restaurant now in The Castro and I have my own studio apartment."

"Why didn't you contact us?"

"I wanted my debtors to think I was dead, so I waited a year. Out of sight, out of mind. In the meantime, I got a new social security card using the name John Smith. You'd be surprised how easy it is. I'm almost my old self. I swear."

He stopped talking and after awhile I asked, "So what do you want from me? Brad and I are committed to each other. I love him with all my heart and soul."

"I don't want to be your lover. I've met someone who loves me and I love him. I just want to be in your life and prove that I have changed. I can be as good a friend as you once thought I was. I did care for you. I swear."

"Once I thought of you as a lover, never just a friend," I commented. "You ruined that love with greed, drugs, and lies. Speaking of lies is Jorge still alive."

"Who knows? He was heavily addicted and he left me when I ran out of money. His addiction was my fault too. I can't make amends to him, but please let me try making amends to you and Brad."

"Brad would never trust you. I don't think I can either, but I'll talk to him and get back to you. If he doesn't want to give you another chance, please don't contact me again. Give me your telephone number and I'll call you in a couple of days, one way or the other. Now please get out of here. I've got work to do."

Carl looked crest fallen but he gave me his number and left without another word.

We had furnished the third bedroom as an office for Brad, but of course I used it when I needed to as well. The computer was in that room. After dinner I went to the computer to do a lesson on line. Brad had brought work home from the office and he settled down at his desk. After about an hour and a half, we were both winding down so I said to Brad, "Something crazy happened today. I need to discuss it with you."

"Sure," he said. We wrapped up our work and went into the living room. I hardly knew how to start so I took a deep breath and plunged right in. Brad sat facing me with his jaw dropped in disbelief. To his credit, he did not interrupt me even once.

When I finished there was a long silence. Finally Brad said, "Not in a trillion years would I let him back into our lives. He's a no good skunk and that's all there is to it. He might have fooled you, but I don't trust him."

Very quietly I said, "I know how you feel and you are right, but I saw him. He's healthy and he has a good job. He doesn't want to come between us. He just wants our friendship. He told me that he has a lover. What he needs are friends, even one good friend. Do you doubt my commitment to you?"

"Of course not, love. What I doubt is his sincerity."

"He doesn't know where we live, although he could easily find out. Suppose we have dinner where he works and we can talk to him there. At least give him a chance for my sake, and for old time's sake. If you still say no after that, I'll respect your wishes and tell him to get lost."

"I can never say no to you," Brad said as he threw his arms around me. Call him and set up something for Friday evening."

Carl, or I should say, John, was very emotional when I called him and I thought I heard a sob. Friday was agreed upon.

Brad and I kissed passionately and he asked, "Do you think you can make love to me tonight without fantasizing that I'm him?" Brad was obviously still jealous.

"Of course I can," I answered him. "It's easy. His cock is twice as big as yours. I could never get them mixed up." Brad slapped me on my rear as he chased me to the bedroom.

Brad's jealously worked in my favor. On special occasions, when we had something to celebrate, one of us would remain passive and the other would do all the love making. Brad was determined to make love to me tonight so that no other body could take his place or enter my mind.

His feather like tongue found every inch of my body. He rimmed me until I was clutching the sheets in ecstasy. When he exhausted every other inch of me, he concentrated on my cock. He teased me for what seemed like hours, but was only a few minutes. He prevented me from cumming and I wanted to scream. Finally, he lubed my cock and his ass and he sat down on me pushing my cock into his slimy ass. I came after only a couple of strokes.

When we lay side by side, trying to get our breaths back, Brad said, "I'll bet the druggie can't do that for you."

"Even if he could, and I doubt it, it will always be better with you," I said. I leaned over and kissed Brad before we fell into a deep and contented sleep.

Brad did something behind my back, but I couldn't fault him. He called our dads and told them about John Smith. He asked them to please join us for dinner and give us their objective opinion about the change or lack of change in Carl.

When the four of us entered the restaurant, John Smith was taking an order. He looked up, and when he saw that there were four of us, I could see the look of surprise on his face. We requested to be seated at John's station, and the host was happy to oblige.

When John came over to our table, he had a pitcher of water in his hand and after he filled our glasses, he asked if we would like a drink before dinner. We all ordered wine and he started to leave. I grabbed his arm and said, "Hold it a minute, Ca...John." I extended my hand and he shook it. "You know Brad," I said. He held his hand out to Brad who ignored it. "This is Larry and this is Chuck," I said. Larry and Chuck are our dads." John looked surprised. They both shook his hand, and he left to place our orders.

After he served the wine, John took our dinner orders. He was very busy and we didn't see him again until he served dinner along with fresh rolls.

"I spoke to my boss," he said. "I told him that you guys were very old friends and he said that when you were finished with dinner, I could take a few minutes off to talk to you."

"Terrific!" I said.

By the time we finished dinner, the restaurant had cleared out considerably. I had the feeling that John had served us slowly so that we would be virtually alone in the restaurant. As we were drinking our coffees, he pulled up a chair and sat down with us. There was a very awkward silence and finally John said, "Explain how Chuck and Larry are your dads, Aaron. It looks like you have a new family. I sure wish I had a dad who wouldn't toss me out of the house."

That did it. As he said that, I could see a look of pity cross Larry's face and he laid his hand on Chuck's. I declined to mention that Larry was my banker. I merely said, "Chuck and Larry are our neighbors and they have adopted us."

"That's great," he said. "Look guys, I am not looking to disrupt anyone's life or to intrude. It's just that Aaron and I were good friends once, and I fucked up that friendship as royally as anyone can. All I'm asking is a chance to prove my sobriety and ask for your friendship. I'm going through hell right now trying to stay sober and rebuild my life, and I sure could use some friends."

Brad was the first to speak. "How do we know we can trust you? How do we know that the guy in the car wasn't your partner in crime, and you were just lucky enough to jump out of the car before it tumbled over the guard rail? You have lied so many times before, how can we believe you this time?"

"Just before I sat down at the table," John said, "I made a phone call. He'll be here soon and he'll try to vouch for me."

"Who is it?" Brad asked. "How can we trust him?" Just then a tall, distinguished looking man approached our table. John jumped up and squeezed in another chair. We all recognized the newcomer immediately and we stood to greet him with a handshake and a peck on the cheek. It was Reverend Clinton Haynes, the pastor of the Metropolitan Community Church, which we all attended. If he was going to vouch for John, we had to listen. Reverend Clint began a narrative.

"Soon after he stopped using drugs, John came to me and told me his entire story. Aaron it was difficult for me to shake your hand every Sunday and keep my mouth shut. I agreed to see John whenever he felt his resolve weakening. Over the past year, his counseling visits have decreased, but his social visits have increased. My dear friends, John and I have fallen in love. I am going to announce our commitment from the pulpit next Sunday morning."

Everyone was stunned. I sure didn't know what to say. I looked at my pastor. He was damned good looking, but he was in his forties, at least twenty years older than John. In my head, I could hear Larry admonishing me some time ago. "Age is just a number, young man. I bet that Chuck and I have a sex life as active as yours." While I was sitting there in a stupor, not knowing what to do or say, my dads jumped up and embraced their friend and pastor and wished him every happiness. Then they embraced John.

What happened next shocked us all. Brad stood up and threw his arms around John. In a loud and clear voice, so that everyone could hear, he said,

"Welcome back to the living, John Smith!!!" I grabbed Brad and kissed him.

"Thank you, darling. I love you," I whispered in his ear.

"Listen up everyone," Larry announced. "Next Sunday after church I want you all to come to our house for a celebration brunch. What do you say?" Everyone agreed.

"How come we haven't seen you in church, John?" I asked

"Clint and I agreed that I should stay hidden until I was ready to face you. Actually I was in the church every Sunday, sitting all alone in the rear of the balcony. I just never went to the social hall after services. I needed Clint and I needed God. I couldn't stay away."

At that point it became hard to say goodnight, but after much hugging and kissing, we parted our ways. Only John stayed behind to finish his shift, help clean up and close the restaurant.

The service that Sunday morning was a joyous celebration of love. Reverend Haynes made his announcement, which was followed by cheering and applause. He asked John to come up to the pulpit where they kissed amidst more applause. Brad kissed me and Larry kissed Chuck and we all had a tear or two running down our cheeks.

The four of us rushed out of church to get things set up for the barbeque at our dads' house. Our dads also invited our neighbors on both sides. Jeanne and Betty were about the same age as our dads, as was the gay couple, Ken and Fred. To our knowledge neither of these couples attended our church, or any church for that matter.

By the time everyone arrived, we had the coals burning red hot. We had set up two picnic tables with sodas, potato salad, cole slaw, hot dog and hamburger rolls, paper plates and plastic utensils. We also had a few beers in the kitchen refrigerator, just in case. It was a simple party, but I just knew it would be a festive one.

Chuck and Larry were perfect hosts. They introduced everyone and in no time everyone was talking to everyone else. The highlights of the afternoon were:

John begged Brad and me one more time for forgiveness. He was so contrite and we had just come from church. How could we not forgive our pastor's partner?

The second highlight: Jeanne, Betty, Ken and Fred were so charmed by Clint that they all said that he would see them in church next Sunday to 'check it out.' As Fred put it, "You are certainly not the typical pastor I grew up with. In my case, you aren't even the typical Rabbi either." That gave us all a good laugh.

I asked John, "When are you two guys moving in together?"

"I work evenings so we decided to start moving some of my stuff over to Clint's each morning. We'll do it slowly a little at a time, but FYI, we are sleeping together every night. God knows, I truly have found out what true love feels like and I don't have to envy you and Brad any more." That called for a major hug.

The afternoon was a total success. We formed even closer bonds to our neighbors, to our dads, to our pastor and to the newly born, John Smith. As we began to bond closer with our neighbors, we began to socialize more. The six of us had dinner together at one of our houses at least once a month.

Thanks to Reverend Clint the others began to attend church most every Sunday morning, and after services we went to brunch together. More often than not, Clint and John joined us. A word about John: Every time I saw him, I could see that he was noticeably improving in health. His cheeks were rosy and his frame was filling out. He no longer looked like a walking skeleton. Obviously he was working out. His muscles were enviable. Once, I delicately asked him about his impotence and he started to laugh.

"When I kicked the habit, I kicked the meds. I assure you I make Clint very happy in that department."

As idyllic as everything seemed, I kept waiting for John to fuck up in some way and disappoint us all. I was so expecting it to happen that I think I would have been disappointed if he didn't fuck up. Listen to me. I would be disappointed whether he fucked up or whether he didn't. I was acting crazy enough to wonder if my aneurism had recurred.

I didn't have to wait long for the shoe to drop.

Brad was scheduled to sit for the CPA exams at the end of the month. It is a grueling three day exam given on a Wednesday through a Friday. In order to avoid all diversions, we agreed that Brad would check into a downtown hotel on Tuesday afternoon and check out on Friday. We agreed to talk to each other briefly for a few minutes each evening that we were apart, but Brad was to concentrate solely on the exams. All of our friends were aware of our plans and agreed not to call us during the exam period..

What we were unaware of, was that Clint was going away on a three day retreat at the same time as Brad's exams. John and I would be without our partners for three days, but in all fairness to me, I knew nothing about the retreat.

John usually got home from work about 11 PM after the restaurant closed. I usually went to bed no later than 10 PM because I awoke at 4:30 AM. I had gone to bed about 9:30 PM on the first night Brad was away. I called his hotel room. Of course, he was studying hard. I told him how much I loved him and wished him well. I wasn't able to fall asleep that night because I wasn't used to sleeping alone, so I decided to watch the ten o'clock news for awhile.

At about 10:35 the door bell rang and it was persistent. It sounded like someone was leaning on the bell. I ran down stairs wearing only the sexy boxers Larry had bought for me after the drug dealer had stolen all my clothes. I opened the door, and there stood John grinning at me sheepishly.

"You look as sexy as ever in those shorts," he said to me. I was too shocked to say anything. He pushed past me and closed the door. Then he grabbed me and began to kiss me. I started to resist, but old memories came back and after a few seconds I began to respond to his kisses.

Finally I pulled away and asked him, "Isn't Clint expecting you?"

"Nah! He's on a retreat," he told me, "and I am one horny son of a gun."

"Please leave," I begged.

"You know you don't want me to leave," he answered me.

"You told me that you were HIV positive," I won't risk it.

John, nee Carl, started to laugh. That's when I was looking for sympathy from you and Brad. I was lying. I'm clean as a whistle. Ask Clint."

"Don't you love him?" I asked.

"Of course I love him. Remember I told you that love was a commitment but sex was for fun. I'm here to have some fun."

He encircled me with his powerful arms and resumed kissing me. He rubbed his massive rod against my already stiff cock, and all my reserves melted.

"Yes, let's have fun," I said as I led him into the bedroom.

- Chapter Eleven -

John threw me roughly on the bed. He laid me on my back and ripped my shorts off.

"Nice," he said as he viewed my hard cock. Clint's a little on the small size."

He began to disrobe quickly. He was not wearing any underwear and soon his massive, erect cock came into view. I had forgotten how big it was and my mouth began to water in my desire to devour it. John straddled my body and crept up until his balls were tickling my chin. He aimed his cock at me and brushed my lips with his cock head.

"Take it," he said. "I know how good you are. I taught you."

I wanted it so badly. My mouth began to open without my willing it. I grabbed his cock and started moving it toward my waiting mouth. Suddenly I turned over knocking him off me.

"No," I yelled, "I can't do this. I can't cheat on Brad."

"I know you want it," John purred.   Besides nobody will ever know."

"I'll know," I sobbed.   "I'll know.   Please Carl (I called him Carl) get out of here and leave me alone."

"No," he said, "I won't go. I know you want it as much as I do." He grabbed me and turned me on my stomach. He was so much stronger than I am that I couldn't wriggle away from him. He pinned me down so tightly, I could hardly breathe. And then I felt it. His cock was at my crack. He was going to enter me and I was helpless. He was going in dry and I was scared.

I screamed in pain as his oversized cock invaded me. He didn't wait for me to get used to him and he started pumping immediately. The pain was more than I could bear and I passed out.

When I awoke, I was alone. I was struck by how quiet the house was. The bedroom lights were on and I could see the clock on Brad's night table. It was 2 AM. I had to get up for work in two and a half hours. I wanted to move but I couldn't. I felt something sticky cementing me to the bed. I reached down and put some of the sticky substance on my finger tips.   I looked at my fingers and they were covered with coagulating blood. I was lying in a pool of blood and in excruciating pain.

With the greatest effort I have ever exerted, I crawled up my bed until I could reach the telephone on my night stand. I punched in my dads' number. Their phone rang several times, but eventually Larry answered and I knew that I had awakened him. I could tell that he wasn't quite sure yet where he was.

"Who is it?" he asked. He was obviously still too much asleep to read his caller ID.

I tried to talk and didn't realize how difficult it would be. Exerting even more effort I said, "I need you." It was all I could mutter because I passed out again. I didn't realize it at the time but I was bleeding to death.

I thought I was back in Ft. Lauderdale after the bus accident. I was certain that I was in a hospital as I slipped in and out of consciousness. This time I was vaguely aware that I was in a private room. I don't remember any doctors or nurses attending to me. Did my loved ones come around? I didn't know.

I became aware of reality early Friday morning. I could see that I was receiving a blood transfusion and a saline IV. Damn it, I had a catheter in me. A beautiful young nurse came into the room. When she saw I was awake, she smiled broadly at me. Both her cheeks became dimpled. I knew that if I was straight, I'd be instantly in love with her.

"Well, if it isn't sleeping beauty," she said. "Your visitors start coming around after work in the late afternoon. Until then you'll have to put up with me. Now," she said, "I need to bathe you so you'll have to help me."

This was my third serious hospital visit in a little over two years. I knew the routines well. I couldn't help but wonder if this was to be my life, being a patient in a hospital every few months. This time, however, I was wracked with guilt. This time it was entirely my fault. I had led John to believe he could have me. He was too far gone in rapture to obey my wish to stop.

I let the nurse do what she had to do but I was in a robotic state. I could hardly understand the doctor when he told me that my colon had been ripped and he had to stitch me up. The stitches would dissolve in a few days and they were healing nicely.

At about noon, Chuck came in. He had no classes that afternoon and he rushed right over. The first thing he did was to call Larry and tell him that I was awake. I started to cry and asked him if Brad knew.

"No, we didn't tell him. We just told him that you didn't want to divert his attention one iota from his exams, and that you wouldn't talk to him until after the last exam. The last exam ended at noon so he'll be calling you soon. Here's your cell phone." He laid it on the cabinet beside my bed just as it rang.

"Hi honey," I heard Brad's cheery voice. I need to stop at the office and then I'll go straight home. Do you think you can get away a little earlier today?"

"How did it go?" I asked.

"Are you OK? I can hardly hear you."

I tried to speak up. "Yes, I'm fine. You didn't answer me. How did it go?"

"I'm pretty confident about things. I'll tell you all about it later. I love you."

"I love you too."

"Don't worry," Chuck said. "Jamie and Jim are going to tell him about your rape and send him to the hospital. Larry and I cleaned up the bloody sheets and put fresh linen on your bed so he won't have to see that."

I started to cry. "Oh Pop, it's entirely my fault. I should never have let him in the house."

"It was not your fault. Don't ever think that. Carl or John or whoever, was never any good. You forgave him once too often. That's the only thing you are guilty of. It's Clint I feel bad for. John has taken off and nobody knows where he is. If you press charges, he'll be wanted by the police and that's a whole other ball game."

"I won't," I said. "He'll only say that I encouraged him and there's a little truth in that." I began crying again and Pop cradled me in his arms.

"I've got to pee," I said. That surprised me because I had a catheter. I looked down and saw that the catheter was gone. The doctor had removed it and I hadn't been aware of it. There was a urinal on my bed stand and Pop handed it to me.

"I wonder if I can go to the bath room."

"Let me ask the nurse," Pop said. He was back in a jiffy with the cute nurse. They both got me out of bed and I had no trouble walking to the bath room.

"If you need to do the other," she said, "don't be afraid. We gave you stool softeners with your meds." I was glad to hear that.

I realized that I was feeling pretty good. I had no pain. There wasn't any bleeding, and they had stopped my transfusions. I really wanted to go home. The only fear I had was facing Brad.

Sometime in the mid afternoon, the doctor came in to tell me that he had written orders to discharge me the next morning. He also advised me, that given the circumstances, I should be tested for HIV in about two weeks. I was ecstatic about going home, but filled with fear at the same time. What if Brad wanted to kick me out? I had acted badly enough. I wouldn't blame him.

Before long, Brad came rushing into my room. He was crying as he took me into his arms and cradled me against his chest.

"I swear, I'll kill that bastard. I'll kill him. How many times can he destroy your life? I'll never let him near you again. It's my fault. I didn't want you to meet him at the restaurant and I let you do it. How could I have been so dumb?"

That was odd. Brad was blaming himself and I was blaming myself. I had to say something.

"Stop it Brad. It's nobody's fault. He's no good and I was too willing to give him the benefit of the doubt. The doctor says I'll be fine. It's Reverend Clint we should be concerned about. He won't be back from his retreat until tonight.

Brad knew nothing about the retreat so Pop and I filled him in. Just then Larry came into the room and he was crying like a baby. "This crying has got to stop," I said. "The Pacific Ocean is rising and San Francisco is in danger of flooding." That lightened the mood and got us all laughing.

"I left a message on Clint's home phone for him to call me as soon as he gets home. He doesn't know anything about this yet," Dad said. Then he looked at me. "Aaron," he said, I want Clint to tell us what he knows about Carl's HIV status. It seems everyone was reverting to calling the rapist, Carl. The name John was reserved for the good guy.

I really was not very sick at this point so we all went into the visitor's lounge at the end of the hallway. The four of us could sit comfortably there and talk.

"I want to hear all about the exams," I said to Brad. "I won't let you put it off any longer."

"All I'm going to say is I think I passed all the sections, but I don't want ever to talk about it again until I get the official results."

Pop asked, "What do you say I go out and get Chinese food for dinner? We can eat it here and Aaron won't have to eat the hospital garbage." We all thought it was a great idea, and our dads left us to get the food.

The minute they were gone, I confessed to Brad that I had almost weakened, and that for a brief moment, I wanted to have sex with Carl. When I got my senses back, he wouldn't stop, and I wasn't strong enough to stop him, so he raped me. I shut my eyes expecting Brad to berate me. Instead he took me in his arms and held me tight.

"That's why I'll never let him near you again," Brad said. "He's like the serpent in the Garden of Eden and you're like Eve. Every time he appears, he tempts you into evil. I know it's a spell he has over you. I can't fight the spell, but I can keep him away from you so that he can't cast his evil spell on you, ever again. You fought him this time and it cost you dearly. In some ways I almost wish you had not resisted him. He might not have hurt you then."

"We don't know that," I answered. "I'm glad I said, no!"

Just then someone came into the lounge and turned on the television. The evening news was on and I for one paid no attention until I heard Brad yell, "Holy shit!!!" The other guy in the room and I turned our attention to the television. In a small town about one hundred miles south of San Francisco, a young man had attempted to rob a convenience store. His face was clearly visible in the surveillance tapes. It was John Smith.

One of the customers in the store was an off duty cop. He pulled his gun and John surrendered immediately. The gun he was using for the robbery was only a toy. As soon as the police officer replaced the gun in his holster and attempted to handcuff the perpetrator, he made a run for it. The policeman retrieved his gun, ran after the criminal and shot him once in the arm and once in the leg. Ironically it was the same two limbs Carl had broken in the bus accident.

Brad and I were left with mouths agape. "I guess we can count on his being put away for a few years. A good looking guy like him should get plenty of action in jail," Brad observed. "Good riddance is all I can say."

I was speechless. When our dads returned, we told them what we had just seen, and Dad commented that when Clint called, it was going to be harder and harder to tell him everything.

The aroma in the lounge was wonderful. I had only been fed by IV for almost three days so I dove into the food. There was so much food that Pop asked the other guy in the room if he'd like some, and he gladly accepted. We were having a joyous evening. Jim and Jamie stopped by on their way home to wish me well, but they only stayed a few moments. By the time our dads were ready to leave, they had still not heard from Clint.

Brad refused to leave me, and talked the night nurse into letting him camp out on a chair. I begged him to go home but he wouldn't hear of it. Just about midnight, I felt someone take my hand. At first I thought it was Brad, but I could see him snoozing in the chair.

The presence was aware of my disorientation and said, "Aaron, it's me, Clint."

That woke me fully and rather quickly. I sat up in bed and we embraced. It was funny. We both said the same thing at the same time. "I'm so sorry!"

"I guess he fooled me," Clint said. "And I guess he fooled you a lot of times. He was so sincere about repenting, about finding God, about loving me."

"Don't be so hard on yourself," I said. "I've known from the start that the only one Carl loves is Carl. Still I let him use me every time and prayed that I could get him to love me. I'm the dumb one. He fooled me three times."

"Tomorrow I'm going down to the hospital where they're holding him. He'll need help," Clint said.

"Are you insane?" Brad yelled at the Reverend. "He'll beguile you again, just as he's beguiled Aaron over and over again. I beg you to let him be and write him out of your life."

"I know you mean well and your advice is heartfelt and sincere, but he's a human being in trouble. I can't just abandon him. All I can do is to keep him from enchanting me again."

I could hear Brad sigh loudly. "I have failed in keeping him away from Aaron. Why should I expect that I could deter you, Reverend Clint?"

"You can't," Clint said. "Aaron, I just wanted to tell you how sorry I am before I leave. Brad, take good care of Aaron." He left abruptly. As soon as he left, Brad stripped to his shorts and joined me in bed. Now we could both fall asleep peacefully.

I healed quickly, and our routine life resumed except for one thing. Even though I was fully healed, and the doctor gave me the go ahead, I would not let Brad fuck me. God knows I wanted him to, but I cringed at the thought. Besides that, even though Carl had assured me that he was HIV negative, I wanted to wait for a test. Thank God, I was negative.

Eventually Brad came up with a solution. He would insert one well lubed finger up my ass for as many nights as it took. He would try to stroke my prostate and get me excited there again. When I was comfortable with that, he would use two fingers. Little by little he would increase the number of fingers until his cock was no bigger than what he had in me.

In less than a week, his fingers were massaging my prostate to the point where I actually had an orgasm. After that, I said to Brad, "I think I'm ready." The very next time we made love, Brad fucked me. He was gentle, slow and very careful not to hurt me. I tried to wipe out the vision of Carl's rape, and soon having Brad inside of me brought back all the old joy I used to feel.

Brad had fucked me from the rear. When he was finished he lay on top of me. I think he was afraid to move. "I'm fine," I assured him, "and have I told you how much I love you."

"You might have," he said, "but I could hear it over and over again."

The first Sunday after I got out of the hospital, we did not go to church. I was still weak and healing. The next Sunday, we did attend services and stayed afterwards to speak to Clint. Obviously we wanted to know how things went with Carl.

"At first he wouldn't look at me," Clint said, "but after awhile, he started to sob. He told me how sorry he was. He didn't know what had come over him, and it would never happen again. He grabbed my hand and begged me to speak to the court to have him remanded into my custody for a probationary period. He was so convincing that I thought that might be a good idea. I told him that I would try.

"I went down to the local police station and found the cop who had shot him. I asked about the possibility of having him transferred into my custody since it was a first offense. The policeman laughed at me. He had pulled his record under his real name in San Francisco and Ft. Lauderdale. He had a long docket of arrests in Florida for drugs, robberies, assaults, and batteries.

"In San Francisco, He was arrested twice on drug charges under the name Carl Gilmore and several times under the name John Smith. The dates of the John Smith arrests spanned the time I was counseling him. He was as big a con artist, Aaron, as Brad has been telling you all this time.

"I walked out of the police station and out of his life. I hope he does go to jail. It's the only chance he'll get to become clean and sober. I decided then and there that the way to help him was not to."

We both hugged Clint and left the church. Our dads and our neighbors were waiting for us to go to brunch. We filled them in on Clint's visit to Carl. "Please," I begged everyone. "If he ever shows up and tries to convince you that he is a changed man, run away as far and as fast as you can."

- Chapter Twelve -

After brunch, Brad and I rushed home. Somehow Clint's story about Carl seemed to mark the end of him in our lives. He was completely out of my system and I intended to show Brad by making love to him like never before.

As soon as we got in the house, I drew all the blinds on the ground floor windows. We and our dads had a signal. If the blinds were drawn in either of our houses it meant "DO NOT DISTURB," hanky panky in progress. Even though we had showered just before church, I insisted that Brad take a shower with me.

"This time I do all the work," I told him. He started to object but I hushed him. We disrobed quickly and I started the shower. We waited until the temperature suited both of us and we entered the stall. I wouldn't let Brad do a thing. I started by shampooing his thick, ash blonde hair. Then I took a wash cloth and got it good and soapy. I began to wash every part of his body, starting tenderly at his face and working down. I washed his ears and then ran my tongue all around the inside and outside of his ears. Brad shivered under the hot water.

I soaped his torso, nipping playfully at his nipples. I turned him and washed his back side. I took plenty of time washing his butt and his crack. I got on my knees and kissed his cheeks and then my tongue sucked playfully up and down his crack. Every once in a while I stuck my tongue into his asshole as far as it would go. Then I inserted a soapy finger and played with his prostate. When he was groaning and squirming I inserted a second finger and then a third.

I turned him again while I was still on my knees, and begin to kiss and caress his balls. He was so hard that his cock kept hitting me on my nose. I could hear the desperation in his voice as he begged me to let him cum. I wrapped my hand around his cock and slowly took it in my mouth. I took him in slowly, a little at a time as my tongue flicked up and down his shaft.

Finally he was entirely in my mouth. I closed my lips on the bottom of his shaft and let my tongue do all the work. I flicked it up and down his shaft as my pursed lips pumped gently at the base of his cock. As I sucked his delicious cock, my fingers played with his crack and his balls.

Suddenly his body stiffened and he yelled out, "I'm cumming my love." I sucked harder as I felt his jism passing through his cock and into my mouth. I sucked out every drop and swallowed every globule. I wouldn't let go of his cock until he begged for relief. I stood up and we embraced. Our bodies pressed together and we were truly united in love.

As we were drying off, Brad said, "You don't think I'm going to let you have all the fun." He took my hand and gently led me to the bed. He repeated everything I had just done, but he wouldn't let me cum in his mouth. Instead, he lubed my cock and his ass. He lay on his back, raised his legs and bade me enter his pleasure dome.

After brunch that morning, we had dropped our dads off before rushing pell mell into our house. They were in a rush also but not for sex (yet). They changed into warm-up suits and set off on a brisk two mile walk to get some much needed exercise. Their path took them past our house and they noticed the drawn blinds.

"Ain't youth wonderful?" Dad remarked.

"It sure is," Pop said. "How about you and I doing a little of that stuff after the walk." As he said that, he winked at Dad and patted his rump. "You're on," Dad answered. Their walk that day was quicker and brisker than usual.

When they got home, they drew the blinds, and headed for the bedroom. They undressed quickly and threw their sweaty warm-up suits into the hamper. Dad turned on the shower and while the water was warming, he was all over Pop. As they kissed with their mouths open and their tongues dueling, they fondled each other's cocks which were stiff and aching.

In the shower they mutually washed each other's bodies, teasing and caressing the other's most erogenous zones. After twenty-five plus years, they knew each other well. When they had teased enough, they stepped out of the shower and dried one another.

As they were drying Pop asked, "Will you fuck me today, Larry? I need you inside of me so badly."

"Your wish is my command, but you better do as much for me." Again they kissed, grabbing and stroking each other's cocks. They lay down in bed in a sixty-nine position. For awhile they just fondled each other's balls and cocks, but after what seemed hours, they tentatively tasted each other in the most teasing manner. But as they got more and more aroused, they took each other all the way in and began to suck their partner's cock, until there was no denying the sensation building in both of them, so they pulled away from each other.

Dad got the lube from his dresser drawer and greased Pop's ass generously and then he obliged his own aching cock. Pop lay on his back and raised his legs, which Dad placed on his shoulders. Dad put his cock on Pop's asshole, and pushed in gently. After years of fucking each other he met almost no resistance. Once in, Dad lay on top of Pop, neither of them moving. They kissed each other with such passion that each began to feel his orgasm resuming. Dad finally began stroking and after only a few long in and out strokes, he came, sobbing on Pop's shoulder. There were tears all over Dad's face and Pop's shoulder.

"I love you so much," each of my dads whispered to each other.

Pop said, "In church today I thanked God for you."

"That's funny," Dad answered. "I did the same. Now stop stalling and fuck me."

"My pleasure," Pop said as they switched positions.

Back at our place, Brad and I were lying naked in bed, trying to recover from our recent love making when the phone rang. I picked it up and it was Reverend Clint. After a few inane remarks, he asked to speak to Brad.

"I need an intervention," he said ironically. "I just got a call from Carl."

"I hope you hung up on him."

"I'm afraid not," the reverend answered. "He told me how sorry he was and begged me to forgive him. He pleaded with me to come to visit him, and by the way, could I bring some cigarette money. I've got to admit, it was hard to deny his sincerity and I began to weaken, but I didn't say I would come."

"If you are really serious about an intervention, the next time he calls, tell him never to call you again and to find himself another patsy. I'd like him to call Aaron. He'd hear a thing or two." I had never seen Brad quite this angry and when he hung up, I had to hold him tight. He was shaking as if we were having an earthquake.

"I hope he get's gang raped in prison," Brad said in a shaky voice. I figured the best thing for me to do was to keep my mouth shut and just comfort Brad. That call ended our romantic mood.

We got up, showered yet again and called our dads to tell them about Clint's call. They didn't answer the phone so we left a message. They called back about a half hour later, and I filled them in. Brad was too emotional to speak of it. Whenever he tried, all that happened was that he hyperventilated.

"I think I'll call Clint and ask him to dinner tonight," Dad said. "He shouldn't be alone. Would you guys like to come also? I'll throw some burgers on the grill."

When Clint arrived he was shaking worse than Brad. "What happened?" Pop yelled at him.

"Just before I left, Carl called again. I told him never to call me again and to find some new patsies. Then I hung up on him. I feel so awful," Clint moaned.

Brad jumped up and put his arms around Clint to comfort him. "Believe me," Brad said. "You did the right thing. You just need time to realize it." All of us kept the make-shift barbeque light and breezy. Carl was not mentioned again, and by the time Clint left, he was in a much better mood.

"We've got to find Clint a boy friend," Brad said, and he did, not too long after that. His need to be a match maker was waking up from a short nap.

I usually got home from work just before five and I never knew when Brad would get home. He was rarely later than 8 PM. A week after the barbeque, I got home and picked up the mail from our box. There was a thick envelope from The California State Education Department. My whole body began to shake. I wanted to rip open the envelope, but I called Brad instead. The receptionist told me that he was out of the office so I called his cell. There was no answer and I thought I would die. All I could do is leave a message.

About fifteen minutes later he called back. "I was in conference with the client," he explained. I told him about the envelope and he begged me to open it. The letter inside was several pages long, but the first paragraph was all I had to read. Brad had passed every section of the CPA exam. While he was hooting and hollering at his end, I read on. Over all he had the highest scores in the state and he had top scores on two of the four sections of the exam. There were detailed instructions of what he was required to do to complete the process of getting his certificate from the state of California. The new inductees were to be honored in a ceremony in Sacramento on November 1, and Brad was to receive a special award honoring his achievement.

"First in the state," I screamed. "You were first in the state. I am so proud of you. I've got to think up a special treat for tonight." I had sex in mind, but as usual our dads had food in mind. Their phone was busy so I ran over to tell them the news. Dad called Brad to congratulate him and to make him promise to be home by seven. Then he called Jamie and Jim, but I couldn't hear what he said to them. I did hear him make reservations for six at a five star restaurant for eight o'clock that evening.

The six of us celebrated in style that night and when Brad and I, and Jamie and Jim, tried to pay, our dads would have none of it. As much as I enjoyed the evening, I couldn't wait to get home and give Brad his dessert.

I wanted to try an experiment this night and maybe I could write about it and get us into the Guinness Book of World Records. I wanted to suck Brad's cock, always stopping before the point of no return to see how many times we could do this before he came spontaneously.

"I don't know about this," Brad said. "It will be pure torture."

"But your orgasm will be mind blowing," I tried to assure him. I was successful eight times, but on the ninth, Brad yelled that he was cumming, and I knew we could delay no longer. He came in my mouth and I could not remember more spunk cumming out of him. He screamed so loud, I expected a call from the neighbors or maybe the police.

"You were right," he moaned. "It was mind blowing."

The next morning at work, Jim called Brad into his office. "I've got some good news all around," he informed Brad. "First of all, I want you to know that you have more than lived up to our aspirations for you. Not only are you an ideal staff person, but you and Aaron are our friends as well. Jamie and I are giving you a substantial raise, in appreciation of how you have helped make this practice grow. We are also going to begin recruiting for another staff person, someone with experience this time. Brad, when we grow to six, I would like you to consider a partnership with us."

Brad was speechless, which was a good thing because Jim wasn't finished.

"Jamie and I want you to do the initial interviews. We figure that you will be working with him, or her, closer than we will. Is that all right with you?"

"Sure, oh sure," Brad was finally able to unlock his tongue.

"I've written an ad for the newspaper," Jim said. He handed a sheet of paper to Brad. "Read it. Edit it if you like, and get it back before noon so we can get it into the gay press as soon as possible and the local newspaper within a day or two." Jim stood up, embraced Brad and kissed him on the lips. Brad took that to mean that he should get back to work.

In his office Brad read the copy:

> *Fast growing CPA firm, with offices in downtown San Francisco, seeks a staff person with a minimum of three year's experience. Our practice is diverse and covers audits in many industries. We also prepare federal, state and local taxes. CPA preferred. CPA candidate acceptable. Send résumé and salary requirements to PO Box 4455, San Francisco, CA 94222, attn: Brad.*

Brad was shocked. Jamie and Jim were going to leave the interviewing to him. This was turning into quite a day.

The ad hit the local newspapers first and Brad received about one hundred résumés, which he quickly weeded down to a dozen. When the ad hit the gay publications, Brad got about twenty more résumés. He spent hours pouring over the thirty-four applicants. He weeded those down to ten, of which four had come out of the gay press, and two were women. One of those four from the gay press intrigued him. The man was a bit more mature than the other applicants. He was thirty-five and had twelve year's experience. He had been certified in the state of California for nine years. His cover letter noted that circumstances in his private life had forced him to move from Los Angeles and to start over. He was willing to take a salary less than his experience would demand, just to prove himself.

Brad gave the ten finalists' résumés to the receptionist and told her to set up five interviews for him on each of the next two Saturdays. He put his favorite candidate at the top and told her to schedule him last in the day so he would not have to rush the candidate. Brad couldn't wait to meet Russell Wilson and hear his story about why he had to relocate.

When Brad had gone for his interview, he, Jamie and Jim had bonded immediately. After the first four interviews, he felt no such affinity to any of the candidates, and didn't even bring them in to meet Jamie and Jim.

Brad's instincts were right on. When he went out into the reception area to bring Russ Wilson in, he shook his hand and had a vision of this man working side by side with him. Russ towered over Brad. He was at least 6'2" tall. He had straight black hair, blue eyes, and a chin so square it looked chiseled. Underneath his business attire, he was obviously very muscular. To label him as handsome was an understatement.

During the interview Brad asked all the usual questions about Russell's range of experience and he was duly impressed. Then he decided it was time to get personal.

"All the CPA's in this firm are gay," he told Russ. "Does that present a problem?"

"Not at all," he answered. "I'm gay myself."

"You said that you moved to San Francisco for personal reasons. Is it something to do with your professional life? Is it something that I should know about?" Brad knew that Russell would tell all. The bonding had begun the minute they shook hands.

"I don't mind at all," he said. There's really not much to tell. I've known that I was gay since I was a little kid, but I tried to hide it. I'm a big guy so I played sports and dated the hotties in high school, but at night, alone in my room, I had other dreams. Stupidly, I gave in and asked my prom date to marry me. She took my virginity on prom night, while I was dreaming that she was Tom Cruise. Thank God we had no children, but after ten years of marriage, I kept failing in the bedroom and she called me all kinds of names including 'faggot' and she finally kicked me out. I wanted to come out, but I couldn't do it where all my old friends were, so I moved here, and now all I want is a job and a chance to make new friends, preferably gay friends."

"I'd like you to meet the bosses," Brad said.

The five people scheduled for next week's interviews were Brad's least favorites. As far as he was concerned, Russ was his man and he could cancel next week's interviews.

He took him into Jamie's office and they buzzed for Jim. "I'm really impressed with Russ," Brad said, and I'd like you to consider him. He handed them Russell's résumé and cover letter. Jamie read it with Jim looking over his shoulder. They both had the same concern. Would his personal problem impact on the firm. Brad told Russ to tell them what he had told him, and when he was done, Jim said, "In this firm being gay is an asset."

"Why don't I leave you guys alone?" Brad asked.

My guy is so smart. He knew that it was time to talk salary. He left the room, and called me. I don't think I'll be much longer and I think that there is a good chance we have found our man. You'll like him."

No sooner did Brad hang up on me when he was called back into Jim's office. "We think you've made a great choice, Brad." Jim said. Say hello to the fourth member of our group." All Brad could think about was two to go to a partnership.

"Russ is starting Monday. Why don't you show him around the office and call Aaron. It's our treat for dinner tonight, just like we took you guys out when we hired you."

"I'd better not call my dads or they'll show up again," Brad quipped.

"Don't bother," Jamie said. "I'm calling them. Russ should meet our banker and dear friend, and his equally charming partner."

When they were alone, Brad hugged Russ and said, "Welcome aboard. I am so happy for you." Then he showed him around the general office so he would know exactly where everyone and everything was located. Jamie and Jim shared an office and Russ and Brad would share one as well. Brad's office had always been set up for two. They had one more space available as an office for two, but right now it housed file cabinets. It occurred to Brad that they might be looking for more space soon.

"Look," Brad said to Russ, "I don't want to pry into your religious beliefs, but Aaron and I and our dads, who you will meet tonight, go to the gay church every Sunday with some of our neighbors. After church we go for brunch and our minister often joins us. Anyway there is someone there at the church that I want you to meet. I think that you two would like each other."

"Are you trying to fix me up?" Russ asked.

"Yes, I definitely am!"

"Well, thank you then. I appreciate it."

Just then Jamie and Jim joined them. They told them where to meet and at what time that evening. They left Russ and Brad to close the office.

"I have one more thing to do before I lock up," Brad told Russ, "and it gives me great pleasure." He wrote a short memo to his receptionist asking her to cancel next Saturday's appointments.

When they got downstairs, Brad told Russ that there was a hardware store around the corner and he'd like to go there to make him a set of keys for the office. It was only 2 PM when he handed Russ the keys complete with his best wishes.

"How about having a cup of coffee with me before heading home?" Brad asked.

"I'd love to," Russ replied.

They spoke for a good hour, lingering over one cup of coffee. Russ asked about me, but all Brad told him was how we met, and how much we loved each other. He also told him about Chuck and Larry, who had adopted us and treated us like sons, and the great coincidence that Larry was the firm's banker.

Russ spoke of his wife and how she had humiliated him, but how happy he was now.

"Look at it this way," Brad said. "She did you a favor. She forced you to come out and live the life you were meant to live. Do you have anyone, a guy I mean, in your life?" Brad asked.

"I haven't any problems with one night stands, but I really want a relationship like you and Aaron, and Jamie and Jim. It looks like you are trying to help me there," Russ said. "Who is he?"

"That would spoil the surprise. Hey, come to our house tomorrow morning and go to church with us and our dads. It will be much friendlier than you going by yourself the first time."

"I like the sound of that plan," Russ said, so Brad handed him his private card with our home address and phone number."

"It's getting late," Russ said and he got up to leave. They embraced warmly.

"I'll see you later," Brad told him.

- CHAPTER THIRTEEN -

If Russell thought he would feel uncomfortable at dinner, like a stranger perhaps, he was sadly mistaken. It was obvious that the people at the table had forged themselves into a close knit gay family. What was most wonderful, they seemed to be welcoming him to join them. He could almost hear the thoughts of the older couple, "Join us. We have more than enough love to go around."

Much to his surprise and delight, he felt like he did indeed belong to this group of terrific guys. The happiness he felt cannot be described. All evening long, he had to keep himself from crying with joy. The only thing missing for him was a partner. The others were all here with their life partners, and it was obvious how much they loved each other. Somehow, he was convinced that now, as his life was turning around, he would find someone and soon. Poor Russ, he was completely oblivious to the drooling waiters all over the restaurant. Anyone of them would gladly have gone home with him.

As they all stood up to go home, nobody was shy about kissing one another on the lips and hugging each other like bears. Russ was absolutely included in the farewell ritual. Brad gave Russ last minute instructions to our home. He went to his car and we all went to Larry's. Jamie and Jim elected to stay behind for an after dinner drink at the bar.

Sunday morning found Brad acting like a frisky kitten. "What's up with you?" I demanded to know.

"Nothing, nothing at all is up. I just know for a fact that Clint and Russ are going to hit it off big time."

"Well, I'd calm down, if I were you," I told Brad. "I don't want you to be disappointed if it doesn't happen."

"Oh, it will, I know it. You'll see!"

We showered separately. While Brad was in the bathroom performing his morning ritual, I was setting the breakfast table for three. I set up the coffee and took out some frozen bagels from the freezer. They would be defrosted by the time Russ got here.

"Your turn," I heard Brad yell at me. I went upstairs. Brad was still drying himself. Naked or fully dressed, every time I saw Brad, my cock would start to stiffen. Brad started to laugh.

"Not now, stud. We have a guest coming for breakfast." He kissed me and pointed toward the bathroom.

When we sat down to breakfast, Brad said to Russ, "All we're having is coffee and a bagel. You can fill that magnificent body of yours at brunch after church. This is just to hold us over."

"That's not a problem. It's enough just being here with you guys."

Just then there was a knock on the back door which led into the kitchen and there stood Betty and Jeanne, Ken and Fred."

"I just spoke to Larry," Ken said and he told us about your friend Russ here so we just stopped by to meet him before heading on to church, and to wish him good luck at the new job."

As Russ was introduced to our neighbors, he held out his hand, but each of them planted a kiss on his cheek. It was hard to read the emotions on his face. I could see he was surprised, pleased, touched, overwhelmed and about to cry. In twenty-four hours he had gone from knowing nobody in town to meeting a whole slew of new friends. And hadn't Brad promised him that he would meet many others in church that morning?

Chuck drove, and Brad, Russ and I squeezed into the back seat. "Is something special going on at the church today?" Chuck asked as he drove to the far end of the church parking lot without finding a single parking space. Finally he left the lot and we found street parking about two blocks away.

We found our neighbors waiting outside the church with dozens of others. "What's going on?" Fred asked. We were lucky enough to get the last parking spot."

"Didn't you know?" a stranger asked. "Reverend Haynes is performing a commitment ceremony today."

"Wow!" we all uttered.

We rushed into the church to find seats. Russ, Brad and I squeezed into a space which should have been for two. I lost sight of our dads and neighbors in the scramble to find a place. Brad and I watched Russ carefully as Clint came to the altar. He looked particularly handsome this morning. He was wearing white robes especially for the occasion.

"Isn't he hot?" Brad leaned over and asked Russ.

"Hot is an understatement," Russ answered. "In my book, he sizzles."

Brad was reading the church bulletin with today's service. When he got to the names of the two men who were committing, he gave a low whistle. "I know these guys," he said more to Russ than to me. "They're clients. I wonder if Jamie and Jim are here." He looked around, but the church was just too crowded to spot anyone.

After the service and after the commitment ceremony, the congregation was invited to the social hall. The celebrants had provided all the food, and when I saw the spread, I knew that brunch was out that day. Brad took us over to meet the clients who had committed and Jamie and Jim appeared out of nowhere.

"It's nice to see you two atheists here today," Brad said.

"I wouldn't have missed it for the world," Jim answered.

Brad hardly heard him. He was concentrating on looking for Clint so he could introduce him to Russ. It was not until the crowd began to thin that we spotted Clint talking to a group of young men who were gushing all over him.

"Let's go rescue him," I said to Brad. As the three of us approached Clint, and when he saw us, he excused himself from the group and walked toward us. He kissed us both and whispered, "Thanks. Those queens were making me sick with all their false praise. And who is this Adonis you have with you?"

"This handsome man, but not as handsome as you, is Russ Wilson. Starting tomorrow morning, he'll be working with me."

"Lucky you!" Clint said and he reached out to shake Russ's hand. When their hands met, I knew Brad had been absolutely correct. The sparks were flying. The air around us got ten degrees hotter. Something was definitely happening here. Cupid, AKA Brad, had shot his arrows into the right hearts.

"Clint," Brad said. "Russ is hanging out with us this afternoon. "Why don't you come on over? We'll whip up one of our dads' quickie style barbeques for dinner."

Without diverting his eyes from Russ, Clint said. "I'll be there with bells on. Can I bring something?"

"Maybe a couple of six packs of Bud Light."

On the way out of the church, we ran into the firm of Pickler and Underwood and invited them also. To complete the party, we saw our neighbors heading for their car, and so we invited them also. When we finally caught up to our dads, we told them what was happening that afternoon and asked them to stop at a supermarket. We bought hamburger meat, hot dogs, hamburger and hot dog rolls, baked beans, potato salad, cole slaw, pickles, relish, potato chips, and plenty of soda. Brad's little match making efforts were costing us a pretty penny, but we were so happy to do it.

As Brad was getting the fire going in the barbeque, our dads brought over the plastic plates, plastic flatware, and oversized napkins. We had one big picnic table in the back yard, and Ken and Fred carried theirs over with the benches. We had let every couple there know that we were hoping that Clint and Russ would hit it off, and told them to try not to butt in if they saw them together. We needn't have worried. Russ and Clint wanted nothing more than to be alone together. They were huddled together most of the afternoon. A few times I noticed Clint put his hand on Russ and vice versa. I said something to Brad, but he had seen it also.

They were the first to leave and as their cars drove off, I could tell that Russ was following Clint. Hallelujah and amen!

Russ needed no training on the job. He was an old warhorse, but Brad went with him each time he started at a new client, just to introduce him. Most of the client's were gay, and after one look at Mr. Gay America, Brad didn't have to hang around for long, but since they came in one car, he was forced to.

Russ confided to Brad that he and Clint were spending a lot of time together and had dinner out once, but they had not yet had sex. They wanted to make sure it was the right thing for them.

"Clint told me about John or Carl or whoever, and I don't think he's over him yet," Russ said. "That's why I don't want to push sex until he's sure of me."

"Very wise," Brad agreed. "Aaron had a difficult time getting Devil Carl out of his system, and it negatively impacted on our relationship. Sometimes I think Carl could still talk Aaron into trusting him and helping him out. You're doing the right thing to wait for Clint to exorcise the demon."

"We have a date Friday night," Russ said. "Dinner and a movie. I'm really hoping he makes a move on me. I am so ready."

Having dealt with the effect Carl has on people, all Brad could mutter was, "Good luck!"

Friday night rolled around and Clint was busy getting ready for his date with Russ. He knew that if he wanted to, they could have sex, no, make love, tonight. Still when he looked at Russ's beautiful face, he could sometimes see John smiling at him. "I'm still in love with that no good SOB, and so is Aaron," he thought. "What's wrong with us? He must have drugged us with a lifetime lasting love potion. I should hate him, not love him. Shit! Shit! Shit!"

In that moment, when he realized how John was ruining his life, he vowed to purge him from his life. He knew my history with Carl, and so he knew that it was easier said than done, but he vowed to be stronger than I was. He also knew that he had fallen in love with Russ and he wasn't going to let anything ruin the purity of that love.

Clint parked his car in front of Russ's apartment. They had agreed that when he got there, he would honk his horn, and Russ would come out. Instead he got out of the car and knocked on Russ's door. As soon as Russ opened the door, he rushed in and Russ closed the door behind him. Clint embraced Russ, and looking in his eyes, he said, "I love you Russ, I want you. I need you. Do you feel anything for me?"

"Oh God! How can you ask me that question? Of course I feel the same way, but I had to wait for you to get rid of your emotional baggage. Can you tell me that you have?"

"Yes, I have. I swear before God. I'm rid of John. Please, Russ, kiss me."

The two lovers skipped both dinner and the movie that night, settling for coffee after the love making. They stripped quickly and examined themselves. They were both hard and Russ had a bead of precum already shining on his cut cock head. Clint was pleased to see that Russ was a little bit on the large size but nowhere near the massive size of John's cock. John had often complained that he wished Clint's cock was bigger. Russ found nothing small about Clint. He was erect and at least six inches, maybe a bit more. He was uncircumcised. "He's just the right size for my ass or my mouth," Russ thought.

They both liked what they saw and embraced, rubbing their cocks together. Russ started to giggle. "I never slept with my pastor before."

"I hope your pastor won't disappoint you," Clint said.

"There's nothing you could do to disappoint me," Clint declared with certainty in his voice.

They coupled three times each that night, making up for lost time, and in Russ's case, making up for bad sex. After each orgasm, achieved by oral sex, they held each other in a vice, reluctant to let go, wanting to meld together. They agreed to wait for another time before having anal sex. Neither had protection or lubrication with them.

"I've never been happier in my life," Russ said.

"Nor I," Clint echoed. "Your cum is the sweetest I have ever tasted. I'll never get enough of it."

"Just keep making love to me like you just did, and you'll get plenty of it. I promise," Russ assured him.

Clint stayed the night and they fell asleep fondling each other's cocks and balls. The first thing Russ said to Clint when he woke up in the morning was, "I love you Clinton Haynes. You're stuck with me and I'm stuck with you, and I like it that way."

"So do I! I've got to say one thing though."

"Uh oh! Should I worry?"

"No it's nothing like that. It's just that when John became my partner, I announced it from the pulpit, and ended up making a complete ass of myself. This time, I won't make any announcements, but I'll be proud to tell everyone I know."

"That's good enough for me," Russ said. "I know who we should inform first."

"Brad and Aaron. Right? Let's call them, and then I have to leave. There is a lot to do before tomorrow's service. I want to make some changes to my sermon."

The phone rang while Brad and I were still half asleep, but I grabbed it and very sleepily said, "Hello."

"Hi Aaron. It's me. Russ. I've got something to tell you. I'm crazy in love with Clint and he loves me right back. We made love, lots of love, last night and we have decided that we want to be together forever. What do you think of that?"

"What took you guys so long?" I said jokingly. I didn't expect to hear the serious answer I got back.

"John, or in your case, Carl. He's what took us so long. I think you are familiar with the problem."

"Yes," I answered more soberly. "I kicked the habit and I take it Clint has also."

"I can only hope that it stays that way for both of you."

I was afraid to answer that last remark. All I could say to end the conversation was, "I'll see you in church."

I turned to look at Brad. He was snoring lightly and he looked so vulnerable and so cute. I wrapped myself around him and started kissing him until he woke up.

"I've got some heavy news for you," I said.

"Is it good or bad news?"

"Good news for now, but only time will tell. Russ and Clint finally made love last night and have committed to each other."

Brad sat up, made a fist, pumped his arm, and shouted, "Yes. I knew they were right for each other."

"What do you think will happen to their relationship when Carl gets out of prison in a couple of years?" I wondered out loud.

"Nothing, they'll weather it, just like we did, just like we will" Brad answered my rhetorical question.

"I hope we can both get by it," I pessimistically commented on the probability of Carl showing up yet again.

"If he ever tries to contact you or Clint again," Brad said with his teeth clenched, "I'll kill him."

- Chapter Fourteen -

The first day of November fell on a Friday. Jamie, Jim, Clint, and Russ all took the day off to drive to Sacramento to be present when Brad got his award. Of course our dads, Brad and I went in a separate car. No speeches were necessary, but Brad did take a moment to thank the State Education Department for this singular honor.

By Monday morning, he had framed the document and it was hanging over his desk with his CPA certificate and his certificates of membership in the AICPA and the California State Society of CPA's. Russ had the same certificates hanging over his desk, but not the one for having scored the highest grades in the state. Nobody in the office was jealous. They all had a deep sense of pride. It was as if the achievement of any one of them was the achievement of all of them. The walls of the entire office were hung with certificates of achievement and other civic and academic awards. Only the secretary and the receptionist gushed over Brad and his great accomplishment.

Both the Thanksgiving and Christmas Eve holidays were celebrated at our dads' house. In addition to us and the neighbors, they had Clint and Russ, Jamie and Jim, Matt, the nurse, and Brad's friends, David and George.

There was a Christmas Eve service at our church so we could not begin our celebration until about 10 PM. It was to be very short. We would exchange token gifts and toast the reason for the season. Our dads assured everyone they would be home by midnight.

We had exchanged token gifts on Christmas Eve, but on Christmas morning, we went to our dads' house and exchanged our real gifts. We then went to services. Clint was in rare form that morning. He extolled the power of love, and reminded us that love was the message Jesus had delivered. "Nowhere in the scriptures," he reminded us, "does it say that Jesus hated anyone for being different than he was. Remember," Clint concluded his sermon, "love yourself, love your neighbor and especially love your enemy."

After those last words, I could see Brad wince. I guess Carl was his enemy and he just couldn't love him, no matter what. I was more at peace with the Carl situation. I had come to the conclusion that I could forgive him, but I could never again trust him. I was certain that he would reappear after he finished his jail term. After all, he had no place else to go. I had no idea how I would handle myself when that day came. I wanted to discuss it with Clint, but I was afraid to.

On New Year's Eve the party would be at our house and could last all night if we wanted it to. We invited the same guests, but some of them had accepted invitations elsewhere. We lost Jamie and Jim, Matt, Betty and Jeanne, and David and George. That still left eight of us, and as far as I was concerned it was just the right size for a party. We arranged for Clint and Russ to sleep over in our guest room. That way nobody had to drive on such a night.

On January fifteenth, I came home and found a message from Carl on the answering machine. *"This is John Smith. Aaron, honey, I need help. I was raped in jail and nobody here gives a damn. I am so afraid it will happen again. I know you don't want to see me, but please get me a lawyer."*

I erased the message so that Brad would never hear it. The next day, I attempted to reach the warden at Carl's prison. I couldn't reach him at first, but he was kind enough to call me back on my cell phone. When I expressed concern that John Smith had been raped, the warden started to laugh.

"You've got that a little mixed up, sir. John wasn't raped. He was the one who raped a new inmate literally minutes after he was brought in. We allowed him to make up to three phone calls and he's now in solitary confinement. They will be bringing him up on rape charges if I can persuade the kid he raped to press charges. If he goes to trial and gets convicted, he'll be here a very long time."

"Thank you, sir," I said and hung up. One of my counter men was looking at me strangely so I said to him, "Feel free to kick me in the ass. I've made a jackass out of myself once again."

I called Clint, and told him all about my call from John and my call to the warden.

"You just saved me a call," Clint said. "I got the same phone call from him, and I was just about to call the warden. I wanted to wait until Russ went to work. It looks like he'll never change. What do you say we neglect to tell Russ and Brad anything about this?"

Out of curiosity I called the warden a couple of weeks later. He informed me that the young man had refused to press charges against John because he was so embarrassed. "It looks like John will still be released at the end of his term unless he does something stupid again," the warden told me. Again I braced myself for the day I knew John would reappear.

I pictured him crying about how he has seen the light and how he is a new man. He'll beg to be put up for a few days until he finds a job and finds a place to stay. I imagined myself weakening and Brad stepping in and ordering him away on pain of death. Yes, Brad, I need for you to save me and maybe Clint also.

Late in January, I received notice from the on-line university that I had passed sufficient courses to be advanced to my sophomore year. As had become a ritual in our household, we celebrated by me lying flat on my back naked, while Brad did all the work of bringing me to ecstasy.

During my sophomore, junior and senior years, I was required to do two weeks each year of student teaching. The on-line university made arrangements for me to teach at a local high school just before spring break.

I was going to teach freshman year geometry. Well, I had plenty of time to think about and prepare my lesson plan. After all it was weeks away.

Early in February, I received a call from a Mrs. Bradshaw. She was the regular teacher of the geometry class I was going to student teach. We arranged to meet the next afternoon. I fell in love with Mathilda (Mattie) Bradshaw at first sight. She was a robust lady in her mid fifties. To be kind, the best way to describe her was a bit messy. I don't want to say unkempt. I don't think she had visited a hair salon in thirty years, but when she shook my hand and smiled at me, warmth filled my body. Her inner beauty over powered me.

"How nice to meet you, young man," she said. "I do so admire your tenacity in the way you are earning your degree. It shows real perseverance." She laid out her plans for my two week stint. During that period she was going to introduce the class to three new theorems. She would describe them academically and I would illustrate by doing a real problem on the board. I had the easy part. She had the hard part of lecturing theoretically, but it was a good way to get my feet wet, because to tell the truth, I was scared stiff.

The big day came, and Mattie introduced me to the class. I had it made. The girls all looked at me as if they all wanted to fuck me, and I could tell the gay boys in an instant. They literally drooled. Immediately, I had the attention of most of the class.

Mattie was amazing. I learned a great deal from her. She took a boring theoretical subject, filled it full of jokes and anecdotes and had the class giggling, but learning. If I could have, I would have hugged her right then and there.

"Now," I said to the class when it was my turn, "let's take what we have just been taught and prove it by applying every geometrical theory we have learned so far. On one side of the column, we'll state a fact and on the other side, the theory which proves it." I winked at the class and said, "By the time you have passed all your geometry classes, you will be so logical, nobody will ever argue with you again." The class giggled.

After class it was Mattie who hugged me. "You were wonderful," she said. "You are going to make a great teacher."

I loved the two weeks I taught with Mattie. I fell in love with all the kids. One day, while illustrating a point, I used a little anecdote, and without thinking I interjected the phrase, "My partner, Brad." I realized immediately that I may have erred, but it didn't seem to make much of an impact. Well, it was a school in San Francisco after all.

After class, one of the boys asked if he could talk to me after school and since I had no office, I agreed to meet him in the library at 2 PM.

"Mr. Jackson," he stuttered. He was very nervous.

"Don't be afraid to talk to me. I promise not to bite and definitely not to judge."

He went on. "I heard you refer to your partner, Brad. Are you gay?"

"Yes, I am."

"I am too, but I'm afraid to tell anyone. I know my mom would still be my mom, but I think my dad would disown me. He's always making homophobic jokes, and mocking gays. He has made it quite clear that he hates them. Once I told him that with all that hatred in his heart, Jesus would never let him into heaven. He boxed my ears and said that gays were the ones who would never get to heaven, and he would be there to kick them out if they tried."

"I have friends who came out and their parents said 'so what?' I myself was disowned and excommunicated from my church just a couple of years ago. You never know how it will go. If you aren't ready to come out, then don't. There will come a time when you will either do it or give up a happy life. You'll know when that time is. Do you go to church with your parents every Sunday?"

"Nah," the boy answered. "Mr. holier than thou never goes."

I wrote down the address of our church and told him to be there on Sunday morning just before 10 AM. "I'll be looking for you," I said. "Maybe your questions will be answered there."

After he left, I realized that it was not wise for me to be alone with a student, any student, and I vowed that if Samuel met me in church or spoke to me in school again, I would not be alone with him.

During the two weeks that I taught, I was never happier. Brad was happy for me, and as busy as he was, we made love more than usual. Even though the teaching only took up a couple of hours a day, I took my two week vacation from Wendy's so I could concentrate on it. Brad on the other hand was smack dab in the middle of tax season. He came home late every night and he was exhausted, but not too exhausted for love. I learned what it was to be a tax season widow.

Clint had the same problem, so we decided to have dinner together a couple of evenings a week. Try as we might to avoid the subject, John Smith was always a topic of conversation. We were both convinced that he would show up one day, and we vowed not to see him if possible. We knew he would plead that he had changed and beg us for another chance. We agreed to bring in the cavalry if necessary, in the form of Brad, The Avenger.

That Sunday, standing in front of the church before the service, talking with friends, I saw a bicycle approaching the church. Samuel was riding it. He spotted me immediately and asked where he could park his bike.

"There's a bike stand in the rear," I said. "I'll go with you." I never really expected Sam to show up and had neglected to tell Brad about him. He was looking at me in amazement.

"Come with us," I said to Brad, "and I'll explain." Sam walked his bike to the rear of the church with Brad and me in close pursuit. "Samuel is a student of mine," I told Brad. "He came out to me and he told me that his father told him that all gays go to hell. I thought if he came here, he would see a different picture."

Brad kissed me right in front of Samuel, who smiled at us. "You're an incurable Mr. Goody Two Shoes."

"And you're an incurable romantic."

Once Sam's bike was safely stored, we headed back to the church entrance and I formally introduced him to Brad. "I'm afraid I don't know your last name," I said to Samuel.

"It's Wilkinson," he said.

"Good heavens, that's Brad's name too. What a coincidence," I said. "You know, you two even look alike."

People were still milling about, and I introduced Samuel to our dads and told him that they had adopted us. Our neighbors had already gone inside so I suggested we do likewise. Samuel sat between Brad and me. I wanted to introduce Samuel to Russ, but at Clint's request, he always sat in the first row. I could do that amenity in the social hall after the service.

Clint was right on as usual. His sermons had a way of sounding like he had written them with me in mind. He would have me laughing and crying at the same time. At one point I noticed Samuel trying to hide the fact that he was crying. Clint had the same effect on everyone.

On the way out of the church, we shook Clint's hand and introduced him to Samuel Wilkinson.

"Is this young man your brother?" he asked Brad. "He looks just like you."

"Just a coincidence," I said. Sam's a student of mine." I loved the way that sounded – *a student of mine*.

In the social hall we caught up to our neighbors and Russ chatting together with coffee cups in their hands. Russ came over and kissed us both on the lips. I could see how amazed Sam was. His jaw remained open until he put a Danish pastry in his mouth and started to chew.

We introduced Sam to Russ, who was very blunt. "I can't believe how much you look like Brad," he said.

"It's just a coincidence," I muttered. I couldn't believe how often I had said that this morning. When Clint joined us, he had taken off his robe and was in street clothes. He kissed Russ with an open mouth, and I thought Sam was going to pass out.

Reverend Clint," I said, "Sam is afraid of any consequences he might suffer if he comes out to his parents. I thought you might be able to advise him."

"Yes," Clint answered, "but I have a better idea." He looked around the room and finally spotted who he was looking for. "There's Frank Inman. He's head of our youth ministry. Come with me, young man. I'll introduce you."

Sam and Frank sat on chairs in the corner of the social hall. I could see that they were talking earnestly. When they stood up, Frank embraced Samuel warmly. Sam came back to us and said, "Mr. Inman and I are going to meet for counseling one afternoon a week after school. I'm also going to attend the church's youth group on Friday evenings. Thanks Mr. Jackson. I never would have known about this place if it wasn't for you."

"Is this going to cause problems for you at home?" Brad asked.

"No, my parents don't care much what I do as long as I stay out of trouble. This is my first year in high school. I'll just tell them it's an after school club activity. My dad's too busy to know what's going on anyhow."

"I know what you mean," Brad said. "My dad was out of touch with his family and the world most of the time also."

"Did he drink?" Sam asked. Brad nodded his head sadly.

"My dad used to drink, but he's sober now. I have an old picture of my folks in my wallet," Sam Said. "It was taken when they were very young."

"I'd like to see it," I told Sam. He took the picture from his wallet with much difficulty. It was old and frayed and he handled it delicately.

The picture was indeed very old. There was a handsome young couple holding a little baby. The woman could not have been more than eighteen years old and her husband could not have been more than twenty, and he looked a lot like Brad only his hair was dark and Brad had ash blonde hair. I handed the picture to Brad. He began to shake when he looked at it.

"What are your parents' names?" he asked Sam.

"Anna and Tom," the young boy answered him.

"Is that you in the picture?" Brad asked.

"Oh no, that's my brother. He died before I was born. My father wasn't around when he died, but later on my folks got together again."

Brad grabbed my arm to keep from falling. "Holy shit," he said. "Sam is my brother."

- Chapter Fifteen -

All my family gathered together in the church social hall. Brad had his arms around Sam's shoulders and he was sobbing uncontrollably. Sam looked like he didn't know what hit him. Clint and Russ were trying to get Brad to stop crying so we could plan our next move. My dads and I were just standing immobilized. To say that we were in shock would be an understatement.

"Brad can't just walk in on them," Clint said. "They've got to be given some warning, but what and how?"

Poor little Sam! He didn't know what to say, but he knew he had to say something. He looked up at Brad and asked, "How do you know that you're my brother, and why did my folks say that you were dead?"

"I was just old enough to remember them and to recognize them in the picture. Mom was forced to give me up because she couldn't care for me. I know that it was devastating to her and it shamed her. She probably didn't want you to know about it. I wonder if she told Dad that I died when they got back together. I hope she told him the truth."

Brad reflected on the matter for awhile and concluded that his dad thought he was dead also. If his mother had told him that Brad was in foster care, surely they would have taken him out of the system when they reunited. It was just too horrible for Brad to believe that they would have left him in foster care if his father knew that he was alive.

"What if they don't want to see me?" Brad asked and looked at me.

"That's not an option," I assured him. Any parent would want to see their long lost son. I say, you take Sam home and declare yourself."

"On second thought," Clint said, "maybe that is the best way. If they intentionally abandoned you, they won't have time to make up stories, and you'll know the worst, Brad."

"Come with me, please," Brad begged me.

"Of course," I answered him. We loaded Sam's bike into the trunk of our car, and kissed the others goodbye, promising to call them all later. We started the journey of Brad's life, with Sam directing us to his front door.

When we got there, we took Sam's bike out of the trunk and he walked it up to the front door with Brad and me right behind him. Suddenly the front door flew open and Anna Wilkinson came darting out. She threw her arms around Sam.

"Oh my God! What happened? Did you have an accident? Did these gentlemen hit you with their car?" She was hysterical and slightly incoherent.

"Relax Mom," Sam said. "I'm fine. There was no accident. I just want you to meet someone." He grabbed Brad's hand and took a deep breath.

"This here's your son Brad, Ma, my brother who ain't dead."

Anna fixed her gaze on Brad. She froze in place unable to move. Finally she fainted dead away. She would have hurt herself badly had not Brad and I caught her.

Brad carried her into the house and laid her on the couch. Sam and I went into the bathroom and wet a wash cloth with cold water to place on her forehead.

"She's just as I remember her," Brad said. Then turning to Sam, he asked, "Do you know where your father is?"

"He said he had some yard work to do. He may be in the back yard. I'll get him." Sam ran out and I could hear him yelling, "Dad, come quick, Mom's fainted."

Tom came running into the house with Sam right behind him. I couldn't help notice that he was a handsome man. Brad looked like him, but Tom was bigger and much more muscular than Brad.

"Anna, Anna," he yelled as Brad's mother began to revive. "Are you OK? Tell me that you're OK."

"I'm fine she answered him. I've just had quite a shock." She looked at Brad and said, "Tom, this young man is our son, Bradley." She started to weep again.

"That's not possible," Tom said. "You told me he was dead."

"When you left me, I couldn't take care of him and I placed him in foster care. I was afraid you would kill me if I told you that, so I lied." Again she began to cry hysterically. Sam, Brad and I just stood by helplessly, not knowing exactly what to do.

Tom started to approach his wife in anger, but he stopped short. Instead he walked over to Brad and stood in front of him. He eyed him up and down and then looked in Brad's eyes. Suddenly he cried out, "Bradley, Bradley my son. Oh my God, it is you."

He threw his arms around his son and began slobbering kisses all over Brad's cheeks. Anna and Sam were crying like babies. At last Anna got herself together and stood up. She came up to Brad and started to extend her arms toward him, but suddenly stopped.

"Can you ever forgive me?" she asked.

"I've already forgiven you," Brad said. "This is the greatest day of my life." He went to his mother and buried her in his arms. That got me crying, but I remembered what Sam had said about his father's animosity to homosexuals so I got a hold of myself, and piped in.

"I'm Aaron Jackson," I said. "I'm one of Sam's teachers and a friend of Brad's, a very good friend." Tom shook my hand and said how nice it was to meet me. I loved saying, I'm one of Sam's teachers. I couldn't wait for it to be entirely true.

I made up a little white lie. "When I first saw Sam in school, I couldn't believe how much he looked like Brad. Then I found out they were both named Wilkinson. I knew Brad's history so I got them together. When Sam showed Brad the picture of you that he had in his wallet, he recognized you immediately. I'm so glad I was the catalyst for this reunion."

"Thank you," Tom said, and he joined Anna and Brad in a three way hug.

Eventually everyone composed themselves, and Anna insisted on making a pot of coffee. She dragged out some fresh baked cookies which smelled delicious. Tom and Anna insisted that Brad tell them everything about his life. When he told them that he was a CPA and hoped to make partner soon, I piped in and proudly said that he had the highest score in the state on the CPA exams, and that he was given an award by the State Education Department. They beamed with pride.

"Where do you live?" Tom asked.

"Just a few streets from here. Isn't that wonderful? Aaron and I own a home together."

I didn't imagine it. I saw Tom's eyes became slits.

"You two aren't faggots?" he asked.

Brad stiffened. He walked over to me and took my hand. "Yes, Dad," he said. We're gay, and we are life partners. We love each other very much."

I thought Tom was going to strike Brad, but he restrained himself. Very quietly he said, "I have lost my first born son twice."

That did it. Sam could no longer contain himself. He lost all reason and all his self restraint.

"Stop it, stop it," he yelled. "If you keep on talking like some Stone Age bigot, you are going to lose both your sons. Now be quiet and hear the truth for a change. You have Mom and me living in such fear of your temper, you never hear the truth."

Tom had never heard his son talk like this and he was more than shocked. He sat down on the sofa and said to Sam, "OK, tell me the truth."

At first Sam was silent and I almost asked him if he wanted me to tell Tom what really brought us here today, but he finally regained his tongue. He started with the time he asked to speak with me after class, and how he came out to me. He concluded with today's events at the church, and how they had a youth ministry which could help him.

"The people in that church are not heathens, Dad. They love God and they have love in their hearts. I wish you could meet the minister. He's a good friend of Brad's." Having said all that, he went over to Brad who put his arm around Sam's shoulder.

"We can't help what we are Dad. God made us this way," Brad said.

"Maybe God is testing you," Sam chimed in.

Everything was silent for a moment and then Tom said, "I've done a million foolish things in my life, but I'm not going to be so foolish as to lose both my sons." He held out his arms and wrapped Brad in one and Sam in the other, alternately kissing each on the cheek. In the meantime, I went over to comfort Anna who was non-stop crying.

"What do I call you?" Tom asked me.

"Aaron will do just fine," I answered.

"Is Sam a good student?" he inquired.

"I don't know about his other subjects, but he's a whiz of a math student."

Then he asked Brad, "Is this youth ministry a good idea for Sam?"

"For sure, Dad. I wish I could have been counseled when I came out."

"Me too," I added. "You have no idea how tough it is. I'll tell you my story one day."

After that the conversation drifted away from being gay and gayness to being a family. Tom and Anna began to relax, but sobbed tears of joy intermittently. Sam kept looking at Brad with admiration in his eyes, but all the while he was holding my hand.

Suddenly Sam jumped up and grabbed Brad's hand, letting go of mine. "I want to show you my room," he said and he dragged his big brother upstairs. While they were gone, Brad's parents asked about me. I held nothing back. I told them about my parents disowning me and the hurt that it had caused me. Anna put her arms around me, and Tom said, "That's a shame." He was really coming around. I concluded that his problem was that until today he really didn't know any gay people and judged them by what he had been taught. I told the Wilkinsons about our adopted dads, about Clint and Russ, Jamie and Jim, and the gay family we had created out of our need to have a family. I added that I was jealous of Brad now because he had two families.

I nearly passed out when Tom said, "We're your family now too." And as an after shock, he hugged me. When Brad and Sam came downstairs, that's how they found us.

"I have an idea," I said and excused myself while I went outside to make a call. When I returned, I told everyone that our other dads wanted to meet Brad's family and they were barbequing dinner for us all. "Please say yes," I pleaded.

The Wilkinsons agreed. We gave them the address, and asked them to be there by 5:30, but we would leave now to help get everything ready.

"Can I go with Brad and Aaron, I mean Mr. Jackson?" Sam begged. I guess he thought it was proper to call his teacher, Mr. Jackson.

"Sure," they both said. It took us another fifteen minutes to get out of there with all the hugging, kissing and crying going on. At home, we changed from our Sunday best to appropriate barbeque clothes. Sam had not been really dressed up so he was OK as he was. When we were ready we went over to our Dad and Pop to help get things ready.

"Who else did you invite?" I asked Dad. I knew he would have invited lots of people for the occasion.

"Just family," he said. "Clint and Russ, Jamie and Jim, and we also asked Frank Inman, the Youth Minister. We thought he could talk to the Wilkinsons."

"Great idea," I said.

As all five of us helped to prepare for the barbeque, it began to get dark and very chilly. "I think we should move everything inside," Pop said. "It's too cold tonight. I'll barbeque outside, and you guys can help by bringing everything inside when it's cooked."

It didn't take us long to move everything inside where it was warm and cozy. Pop and Dad had asked all the guests to come fifteen minutes before Brad's folks so everyone would be here when they arrived. It might be a little overwhelming for them, but our dads felt it would be appropriate for them to meet Brad's adopted family altogether.

Brad was nervous and fidgety. He kept looking out the window for the Wilkinsons to arrive. We all tried to calm him down, including Sam, but it wasn't working. Finally they arrived. When Anna was introduced to Chuck and Larry she presented them with a bundle of flowers. I almost had to laugh at Tom. Every time he shook a gay man's hand he looked surprised that his arm didn't burn off. Once he got past that, he relaxed a little but you could see that he was uncomfortable.

If anyone here knew how to relax a guy, it was Clint. He took Tom aside and said. "Your son is one of the finest individuals I have ever met. As his pastor and as his friend, I can tell you that he is one of the few people who live the words of the Lord. You can be very proud of him."

"I didn't think that f… gays even went to church much less had gay ministers. The bible says it's a sin."

"There are prejudices and sins throughout the Bible, like polygamy, slavery, use of non-kosher foods, and the like. You must remember that the Bible was written by men, and it reflected their prejudices and the social mores of their times. However when they wrote down the words of the savior, we know one thing for sure. He preached nothing but love for every body, not just those people he considered to be 'the right people.'"

"Sam said something like that to me once and I boxed his ears."

Clint then steered Tom over to Frank Inman. "Why don't you two talk, so you'll have an idea how Frank can help Sam and counsel him."

Frank took Tom aside as if to preserve confidentially. From time to time, I could see them seemingly lost in deep conversation. Then suddenly Tom began to sob, I mean sob, **loudly**, and Frank cradled him against his chest. Frank kept right on talking to Tom, whispering in his ear. Finally Tom pulled himself away from Frank's chest and I could hear him say, "I know that now, and I will tell my sons, but not tonight. Tonight is a celebration."

I had no idea what Frank had said to Tom, but Tom said he would tell his sons. I hoped that included me. After that Tom was a different person, not only the ease with which he interacted with the gay guests, but I swear, he was warmer and more loving toward Anna. He even went up to Jamie and said jokingly, "My son is the best thing that ever walked into your office. You better treat him good."

"Brad is my brother," Jamie said seriously. "I love him and treat him like I would want to be treated. Everyone who works in our firm is family, Russ too."

"I can see that," Tom said. "You are good people." A tear fell from his eye.

Later on, he asked Clint, "Do you have to be gay to attend your church?"

"Absolutely not! Many parents and relatives of our congregation attend regularly. We even have several straight people who told me that they were tired of the hatred and bigotry they often heard in their churches, and have chosen to join us."

"My family is complete now and in a way, we are a new family. If Sam and Brad are going to attend your service every Sunday, I want to be there with them and Anna."

"You know how welcome you are, and I bet I know three fine young men who will be overjoyed," Clint assured him.

Everyone ate like it was the first meal they had eaten in ages. Anna and Tom spent most of the evening talking to our dads. They laughed and joked and I could tell that the two families were blending. I was so happy for Brad, especially since I knew that my own family would never come around.

At the end of the evening, Dad and Pop would not allow anyone to help them clean up. As everyone said goodbye, there was much kissing on the lips. To my surprise, Tom didn't kiss anyone, but he hugged everybody warmly and told them that he would see them again soon. WOW!

"We live just a few houses down at the corner," I said to Brad's folks. "Please come and see our house before you go home."

"I'd love to," Anna said and we all walked over. They loved what they saw of our David decorated house, but when we showed them our bedroom, Tom said, "I'll never be able to understand how you can do what you do, but I can still love you, and that surprises me."

"Thanks Dad," Brad said. "All we do is show each other how much we love one another in the best way we know how."

"Well, to each his own," Tom said. "As long as you love each other."

It had been such an amazing day, we were all reluctant to end it, so Anna said, "Why don't you guys go in the living room. Sam you come help me. I'll make us some coffee as a good night cap, and you can set up the table in the kitchen. Brad and Aaron you can talk to your father." Another WOW!

Brad, Tom and I went into the living room and Brad took the bull by the horns. "What did you promise Frank to tell us Dad?"

"I'm glad Sam's not here," he said. I wouldn't want him to hear this at his age." He stood up, and faced us both. Then for some reason he faced the ceiling. Without hesitation, but always facing the ceiling, he told us a story.

"Frank made me remember why I hated gays so much. I had blotted it out of my memory. When I was a youngster, my parents often left me with my father's brother, when they went out. Between the ages of eight and ten, my uncle raped me continuously. Finally I had the courage to tell my father. He called me a liar, and said that I was old enough to stay home alone from now on. He and my mother continued to treat my uncle in the same old way and it was never spoken of again. My uncle is in jail right now for raping a slew of young boys. Until they died, my parents would never acknowledge that I had told them the truth. I never forgave them. Tonight Frank made me realize that my uncle was an anomaly, and that not all gays are pedophiles. After all," he went on, "I have two, no three, fine gay sons. Frank even asked me to forgive my uncle and my parents. I did just that, and a great burden was lifted from my heart. He does his job well, even if I'm not exactly a youth." Brad and I put our arms around his father and I know we soothed his tortured soul.

Tom buried his head in his hands and turned away from us, but Brad held him tightly, running his hands up and down Tom's back, soothing him.

Brad whispered in his father's ear. "You know Dad how wonderful it is when a man makes love to a woman, but how horrible and demeaning it is when a man rapes a woman. It was a terrible, disgusting thing your uncle did to you, but when a man loves another man, and they make love, the disgusting act becomes a beautiful thing. Can you see the point I am trying to make? When Aaron and I show each other how much we love the other, we are performing an act of love, but that act can be defiled when it becomes a rape."

Tom gave Brad a peck on the cheek. "I get it," he said, "but please spare me the details." That got us all laughing. We were all laughing hard when Sam called us into the kitchen.

And what of Sam's new life? One of his new friends attended the same high school as he did, and lived only two streets away. His parents knew of his sexual orientation and encouraged him to be part of the youth group at the "gay" church, but Chris could not convince them to come to services. Sam and Chris began to study together and hang out at each other's homes after school. When Chris told his parents that Sam's parents had attended the church, they said that they would give it consideration. Chris was disappointed at their hesitation, especially since he and Sam had fallen in love.

When the boys were still in their sophomore year, I had the opportunity to do my second two weeks of student teaching. This time I taught advanced geometry. Geometry was my favorite subject. To prove all the theorems you had to use pure logic. The intellectual stimulation always excited me. Much to my regret neither Sam nor Chris was in my class.

At the conclusion of the two weeks, the principal asked to see me. He shook my hand warmly, and asked me to be seated.

"According to all the reports I am getting, you have a real talent for teaching and imparting ideas on to your students, ideas way beyond the subject matter. When you get your degree young man, I would hope that you would apply here for a position teaching math. Good math teachers are the hardest to find."

"I'd love to teach here," I said. "It's all I dream of."

After that I worked my ass off. I began to study the minute I got home from work. On my days off, I studied all day, often into the wee hours of the morning. I got very little sleep on those nights.

The one thing I would not sacrifice, for Brad's sake (and mine), was an active sex life. Somehow he and I always made the time to express our love.

It was the summer after the boys had completed their sophomore year that I received word that I had completed enough courses to be advanced to senior status. If I completed my remaining courses by next May, I could get my degree with that year's graduating class at UCSF. I was so excited that I arranged with management to leave an hour earlier every day to work on my courses. I was already training my replacement and we were all comfortable with that arrangement.

All my hard work paid off. After struggling with a raft of administrative paper work, I was set to get my degree at UCSF with that year's graduating class. Unfortunately, I was only given four tickets so I was restricted to having Brad, my dads, and Sam to cheer when they called my name.

But that didn't stop my dads. That evening they made a big party at their house. Brad's family and all our friends and neighbors were invited. Added to the list this time were Chris and his parents, Sarah and Peter Hanson. Anna and Tom couldn't wait to introduce the Hansons to Reverend Clint. Several times during the evening I noticed Clint and Peter deep in conversation. It was going well.

I submitted my résumé and application to Mr. Anderson, the principal at the local high school. The next day he called me personally to tell me that I was hired. He advised me to be available for orientation and meetings beginning about August 15, so I gave my notice at Wendy's effective July 31.

Brad surprised me by booking a gay cruise for the first week of August. I got cold feet at first, but decided it was time to get back on the horse. The cruise had the same itinerary as the one I had missed. When he booked the cruise, he asked to speak to a supervisor. He told her that I had missed a prior cruise due to a horrendous accident. She knew immediately what accident he was referring to. She asked him to hold the line while she checked the records. She was gone for quite awhile and apologized profusely for the delay. Then much to Brad's surprise she informed him that the cruise line was giving both of us a present and the cost of the cruise was on them.

Brad declined trip cancellation insurance for obvious reasons, and elected to take a cab from the airport to the pier instead of the free bus service. I can't imagine why. He booked the flights to and from Ft. Lauderdale and they were about the same times of departure as my original flights. It was too spooky, but I didn't care. I knew Brad would keep me safe and handle everything. What would I do without him?

We had a blast on the cruise. We made lots of friends including two single guys from San Francisco, whom I recognized from having seen both of them at our church. During the course of the trip they hung out a lot with Brad and me, and I think we made a match. By the end of the trip they had slept together, and we couldn't have been happier. They seemed to be so well suited to each other and they were genuinely falling in love. How ironic! That's what I had hoped would happen to me when I booked the original cruise. We all vowed to get together at home, and we did.

As much as I was enjoying the trip, my mind was on getting home and starting my teaching career. That school year, I was assigned to teach my favorite subject, geometry, and my not so favorite subject, trigonometry. As with everything else in life, I was going to have to take the bitter with the better.

Somehow I got through orientation and more piles of paper work. Before I knew it, I found myself showering at a decent hour (after sunrise) in preparation of the first day of school. Brad chose to shower with me, and as a good luck present, he went down on me and teased me until I begged him to let me cum. As much as I love him, he can be an awful tease sometime.

My first class was trig. I walked in to the room shaking like a leaf, but so excited, I could hardly talk. I looked over the class before introducing myself and there sat two brash looking seniors. Sam and Chris were smiling at me like two Cheshire Cats.

- Chapter Sixteen -

I can't tell you where the next year went. One moment I was a quaking newbie walking into my first class, and the next I was, in my opinion, a seasoned teacher.

Jim and Jamie made both Brad and Russ partners right after tax season, and added another man and woman to the staff. Both of them were straight so the professional staff consisted of four gay men, one straight man and one straight woman. The clerical staff remained all straight as it expanded also. Nobody could accuse Pickler and Underwood of being discriminatory.

The firm outgrew their offices and instead of renting a larger space they bought a building with enough space for the firm, with room for expansion, and an additional ten offices for rent. Both the professional and clerical staffs were given the opportunity to invest in the building, but only the professional staff and the office manager took up the offer. Jim and Jamie's first secretary had been elevated to manager, as the firm had grown.

Sam and Chris turned eighteen and declared that their love rivaled Romeo and Juliet, and they were totally committed to each other. They slept with other guys, and one or two girls, just to see how it was. They enjoyed themselves and had fun, but it wasn't right for either of them. They were

totally committed to each other. They both enrolled at UCSF, but both sets
of parents said that unless they could get scholarships they couldn't afford to
send them to the school. Brad and I did not hesitate. We insisted on paying
fifty percent of each boy's tuition and expenses. The parents objected, but
we would not take no for an answer.

"After all," Brad pointed out, "they're our brothers. We have a vested
interest in their future."

The boys chose to live on campus and of course, they were room mates.
They spent the weekends at home in neutral territory – our house. We loved
having them, and their noisy love making often turned us on, and got us
aroused even when we thought that we were too tired for sex.

When the Hansons finally agreed to allow us to help fund Chris's education,
Peter asked us very simply, "Why?"

I wanted to say, "Because I'm loaded," but Brad said, "Our church and our
pastor teach us that giving and charity are the responsibility of every person
on the planet. Aaron and I give as generously as we can to charity, but in
this case the giving begins at home."

"You know," Peter said, "I really liked your pastor when we met him. He's
genuine. Before Chris came out to us, I had all those prejudicial stereotypes
about gays. Little by little, every one is being disproved. Anna and Tom
have been urging us to go to church with them, and you know what? We're
going this Sunday. I'll see you there, buddy."

Brad was so moved he put his arms around Peter and hugged him. Peter
stood almost a foot taller than Brad. Not only did he hug Brad back, but he
put his hand behind Brad's head and held him tightly against his shoulder.

The Hansons attended our church that very Sunday. Clint had them laughing
and crying during the sermon. As usual the Hansons felt that Clint was
talking right to them. They joined us in the social hall after the service and
it seemed to me that they felt right at home. The boys introduced them to
Frank Inman, the youth counselor, and Peter thanked him for a job well
done. It was amazing.

Before I knew where the time had gone, I was sitting with the faculty at my first graduation ceremony. Not that I am prejudiced, but certainly Sam and Chris were the best looking hunks in the senior class. I knew that Brad and I had a profound influence on the boys (should I start saying, the men?), but when Sam said that he was going to major in accounting, and Chris announced that he was going to major in education, I damn near cried.

After the graduation, it was the Hansons this time, who made a back yard barbeque. Besides all of our friends, Sam and Chris invited many of the kids from their youth group.

Alone at home that night, while Brad and I were cuddling in bed, Brad began to play the "What If?" game.

"What if you weren't student teaching in Sam's math class, and what if he hadn't approached you about his sexuality, I never would have met him and I might never have been reunited with my folks," he moaned.

"What if he never attended the youth group at the church? He might never have met Chris," he continued to ponder the wonders of the Universe.

Of course, there were no answers so I played the game myself. "What if my folks hadn't kicked me out and I had stayed in Boise? I never would have met you."

"Stop it!" Brad yelled. "That's too unbearable to think about. Do you ever long to be reunited with them?"

"Once in a while," I mused, "but I know it can never be, so I try not to think of it."

"Why don't you send them a Christmas card this year and see what happens. Maybe you could enclose a short note saying that you are doing well. They might appreciate that," Brad suggested.

"They would never open the letter. You're day dreaming, sweetheart."

Brad persisted. "What about writing to your sisters?"

"That might work, but they're probably married by now and I wouldn't know how to reach them," I replied, remaining negative.

"We could try to Google them or hire a detective. Give me the names and last known addresses of everyone in your family and let me see what I can do," Brad said. Somehow, I got the feeling that Brad was about to embark on an adventure of exploration.

It was summer and I had gotten a job as a day camp counselor at the local YMCA. I also taught evening math classes at the high school two evenings a week. I left for work a little earlier than Brad. The next morning I wrote down the names of my parents and their address and telephone number on a pad, Abigail and Jonathan Jackson. Then I added my younger sister, Marion, who was still living at home when I left. My older sister, Cheryl, was at BYU when I left and that was all I knew.

I went off to work and promptly forgot about it, but at the end of July, Brad came home one day with a grin on his face. He handed me a thin folder and said, "Here's everything you need to know to contact your family. I hired a detective."

Not only was I stunned, I was shaking too hard to take the folder. Brad put the folder on the coffee table in the living room. "Whenever you're ready," he said.

That night as we got ready for bed, I still hadn't looked at the folder, and Brad said nothing. I needed to get my mind off things so I invited Brad to shower with me. He gladly accepted.

Once the warm water was cascading down our naked bodies we began to kiss. I was determined to make this the best session ever. I let my mind fantasize to the first time we had made love, to the first time Carl and I had sex, to the first time Carl, Jorge and I had sex. I was so worked up, I nearly lunged at Brad's cock enveloping it with my lips and gobbling it up. I couldn't seem to get enough of my lover.

"Stop!" he entreated me. "I want to be a part of this. Let's take the action to our bed."

We dried quickly and ran to bed. "My turn!" Brad yelled, and before I knew what happened, my cock was devoured by his mouth, and his tongue was poking at my piss slit. I came suddenly, and he kept right on sucking me, no matter how much I begged him to stop. Eventually the sensitivity wore off and I began to be aroused again by his urgent sucking.

"I'm cumming again," I yelled and spilled more of my seed down his throat.

"Is that what you wanted? Have you delayed enough?" he asked, very annoyed at me. "Now go down stairs and write a letter to any or all of your family. You can also telephone, but I can see that you won't." He turned on his side and faced away from me.

I crept out of bed like a little pussy cat with its tail between its legs and went downstairs. I didn't bother to put a robe on and I was naked. Somehow I was unaware of my state. I stood in front of the coffee table still unable to touch the folder. I was aware only that my cock was sore. Then Brad came up behind me and helped me into a robe.

"Read," he said kindly, and I did.

My mother and father were at the same address and telephone number. My little sister was in college and I had her address and the telephone number to her dorm room, but it was summer now. She might have a different number next semester. My older sister was married and living in Los Angeles. Her husband's name was Adam Bergman and they had one child, a two month old son named Aaron. She named her baby after me? That was too hard to believe. Somehow, I knew that she had not married a Mormon.

I thought about what to do for several days. Brad did not say anything or push me at all. I do so love the guy. Finally I decided to write to Cheryl. She had always been the least provincial of my family. Also she would be the easier of my two sisters to reach. I worked on the letter for two days.

Dear Cheryl:

I know that this letter will come as a huge surprise to you, but whether you reject me or not, I am reaching out to my family. I need to fill a huge void in my life. Truthfully, I am starting with you. Somehow, I feel that you are the one who can be most forgiving in the case of your little brother.

When our parents threw me out because I was gay, I went to San Francisco. I got a job at Wendy's and worked my way up to store manager. All the time I was taking my college courses on line. I finally got my degree in education, and today I teach high school mathematics and I love it. God worked a miracle through me. I was able to reunite one of my students with his long lost brother. It's a long story, and I must save it for another time.

I am partnered with the most wonderful guy in the world. He's a CPA. We own our own home; have two cars; but no children. He has two younger brothers who we mentor, and who we consider to be like our own kids. We are even participating in funding their college educations. Although Bradley has a great relationship with his parents, we have been 'adopted' by an older gay couple who have been more father to us than our own Dad ever was to me.

I would like nothing better than to have a relationship with you and your husband and meet my little nephew. What was his name again? LOL.

I don't ask much. If even one member of my family can accept me and my life style, my life will be complete. I always loved you. I still do. I still love God and go to church every Sunday. It's not a Mormon church, but it's where I learned that God is love.

Please write to me. I have your telephone number. I won't call unless you want me to. I love you.

Your brother,

Aaron.

I mailed the letter two days after completing it. I was still frightened at what might result. It took four days more after that, but I got a reply.

Aaron, Aaron, my beloved brother. Yes, yes, yes! Call me. I yearn to hear your voice. I have missed you so much and (God forgive me) cursed our folks often enough for what they did to you, what they did to both of us.

When I was in college, I worked in a diner on weekends to make extra money. Every Saturday and Sunday morning this gorgeous hunk of a man came in for brunch and flirted with me. He would insist on being seated at my station. He kept asking for a date and I kept saying no. He was a lawyer in a large international law firm. One day he said that he had gotten a promotion and he was being transferred to the Los Angeles office. He said that if I didn't marry him and move to LA with him, he would definitely kill himself. I knew something he didn't. I was so crazy in love with him that if he hadn't asked me to marry him, I would have killed myself. Can you imagine little brother? We hadn't ever been out on an official date and we were talking marriage.

When Mom and Dad heard I was engaged, they showed no joy. Dad only wanted to know if he was a Mormon. When I told him that Adam was Jewish, he did to me what he did to you. He gave me a half hour to pack and get out.

Adam's family lived in Los Angeles and that's why he asked for reassignment there. I took a bus to LA where Adam and his parents met me at the bus terminal. His folks welcomed me with open arms. They paid my tuition to complete my degree in elementary education, and paid for a beautiful wedding for Adam and me. The ceremony was performed jointly by an Episcopal priest and a rabbi. If only I knew where you were. I would have been thrilled to have you walk me down the aisle.

There is a little sad news. Adam's wonderful parents were killed in a plane crash last year. His sixteen year old brother, Ben, lives with us now. Ben has let us know that he is gay and he thought we would kick him out. He should have known his brother better. I can't imagine my life without Ben in it. His kind soul shines through his eyes. Don't tell Adam, but Ben is growing up to be even handsomer than he is. I didn't think that was possible.

Please call immediately you receive this letter. I'll go crazy until I hear from you. I am on maternity leave, so I am home all the time. If you don't reach me at home, my cell number is 323-555-6745.

Love, love, love (give Brad a hug from me and Adam), Cheryl

The minute I stopped crying, I called Brad and read the letter.

"I'm coming right home," he said. "Please don't call your sister until I get there."

Brad was home in half an hour. "OK," he said, "you're on."

I tried several times to dial the number, but I was shaking so badly I kept screwing up and punching in the wrong numbers. Finally Brad grabbed the phone and dialed for me.

A female voice picked up the phone and started yelling. "Aaron, Aaron is that you?" Obviously she had caller ID.

"No, this is Brad. Aaron is shaking too hard to dial. Here, I'm putting him on."

Still quivering, I took the phone from Brad. Quietly I asked, "Cheryl is it really you?"

"Yes, my darling it's me." I started to cry and Brad took back the phone.

"I hope you have lots of time Cheryl," he said. "Aaron can't stop crying."

"Me too," she broke down sobbing.

Suddenly a teen age voice, recently deepened in pitch, said, "Bradley, this is Benjamin. You have no idea how great it is for me to find out that I have two brothers in law who are gay. It's a blast not being the only one in the family. I can't wait to meet you guys. It's hard for us to travel with the baby. Could you come down here for a few days? I don't think Cheryl could bear not seeing and hugging Aaron for much longer."

I grabbed the phone back. "Hi Cheryl, it's Aaron back."

"This is Ben, Aaron. My brother's at work. Wait, here's Cheryl."

"Did you hear what Ben said? How soon can you come?"

"I can give up counseling at the Y for a few days. I teach math at the high school on Tuesday and Thursday evenings. I suppose we could get a late night flight on a Thursday after class and return on Tuesday afternoon if Brad can arrange it." Brad was nodding his head vigorously as if to say, "Yes, I can."

"Let me call you back as soon as we make the arrangements," I said. "I love all of you in LA," I screamed into the phone.

"We love you too," I heard Cheryl and Ben echo back.

Immediately Brad called his office. He told Jim what was going on and Jim gasped, "My God, man. This is so incredible. It's almost like you finding your parents. By all means take as much time as you need."

Then I called the Y and told them I could not be in the following Friday, Monday and Tuesday.

We called the airlines and booked the last shuttle out at 10 PM Thursday evening and an early afternoon flight back on Tuesday. That week I rushed my Thursday evening class because I couldn't concentrate on anything but seeing Cheryl anyway. When I got home, Brad was set to go with our luggage, and our dads were waiting to take us to the airport.

I could barely make it to the baggage claim at LAX. My legs wouldn't support me. As we walked out of the security area, I saw her. Cheryl was more beautiful than I could remember. Standing next to her was Adam, who was every bit the hunk she had described. He was a little over six feet tall. His eyes were blue and seemed to pierce right through me. His chin and his nose seemed chiseled by some great sculptor. His thick chestnut hair was in disarray and tousled all over his face. His body was that of an athlete.

Adam held little Aaron in his arms. He knew that Cheryl and I would want to embrace. Immediately I knew he was one thoughtful dude. Little Aaron looked like a Gerber baby, all red cheeked and blue eyed.

Finally, next to Adam, stood Benjamin. He was a little shorter than Adam but might yet grow taller. He was a clone of Adam, just a younger version.

My eyes devoured the look of this beautiful family, and at last Cheryl and I fell into each other's arms sobbing and kissing. While we were lost in each other's embrace. Brad was making Adam's and Ben's acquaintance.

- Chapter Seventeen -

We were alone in Cheryl's car with little Aaron, who was named for Adam's father, not me. Cheryl told me that she pushed the name on Adam, who readily agreed. Adam, Ben and Brad were driving home in Adam's car. Because of the baby seat, two cars were necessary.

"Marion and I are secretly in touch with each other," Cheryl confided to me. I gave her your address and telephone number and left it to her if she wanted to call you. She also knows that you are with me until Tuesday morning and if she wants to, she can call you here. Obviously she doesn't subscribe to the way we two have been treated, but until she's emancipated, there's not much she can do about it. There is one thing she has rebelled against. Mom and Dad picked out a husband for her and she has vowed never to marry him."

"You know, Cheryl, I never realized what a prison we lived in until the warden released me. Life is so good now. I have no complaints."

"Yes, life is good for me now also. I want to hear all about your life tomorrow. It's really too late now and we should all turn in as soon as we get home," Cheryl sighed.

In the other car, Ben was quizzing Brad about his gay brother, Sam. Adam remained silent, but he was more than interested, and listened intently since this was a sexual avenue he could not explore or help his brother with. The two brothers were fascinated with Brad's story of how Aaron had inadvertently reunited him with his parents and brother, and what a great relationship they all had.

Brad described the predominantly gay church they attended, and the youth ministry which he was able to place Sam in. "That's where he met his present day partner, Chris, and gained all his self esteem," he told Ben.

"I wish I had something like that available to me," Ben lamented.

"I know there are gay synagogues in many cities. Look into it and if you don't find one, I know that there is an MCC in LA. I assure you the youth group would welcome you whether you attend services there or not."

Before Ben could answer, Adam announced," Here we are." He pulled the car up a long driveway and parked behind Cheryl. Then he pushed a gadget hanging from his sun visor and a creaky metal gate closed behind us. Our luggage was all in this car, and the three of us brought it into the house.

Brad and I hung our clothes in the guest room closet and placed our underwear and sox and things in the dresser drawers. We wore underwear for the occasion. We were about to shower in the guest bath when there was a knock at the door. As we grabbed our robes, I asked, "Who is it?"

"It's Ben. Can I come in for just a minute?"

"Just a sec," I answered. I waited until our robes were secured and opened the door.

"What's up, kiddo?" Brad asked.

"I was just wondering if Sam and Chris had an E Mail address and if it would be all right to write to them."

"They already know all about you, and I know that they would love to hear from you. It's a whole month before college starts for them. Maybe your brother would let you come back with us and visit for a bit. Sam and Chris spend more time at our house than at their own anyway," Brad said.

"That would be so neato," Ben said. "I'll talk to Adam in the morning. Thank you so much. I'll let you get some sleep now, *or whatever*." He winked at us as he left the room.

Brad and I were too inhibited to make love either in the shower or the bed, so we resigned ourselves to a sexless week. How wrong we were. Every night we managed to have oral sex. We stuffed our mouths with a pillow to muffle our screams, and maybe we got away with it.

Adam arranged to take a few days off from work, and we spent the weekend sightseeing, going to the beach and bonding as a family. Adam secured Ben a ticket on our flight back to San Francisco with a return to LA on Labor Day. That was the only day he could get a seat because of the holiday. It was a late evening flight so Ben could enjoy Labor Day with us and he would be with us for two whole weeks. I alerted Sam and Chris to please make some time for him.

The two young MEN were winding down their stay in the Youth Group. It would be the end for them when they started college, but they intended to take Ben to their final meetings and introduce him to a particular young man that they had in mind for him. I hadn't realized before, but they had a talent for matchmaking. Since Sam is Brad's brother, I figure that the apple doesn't fall far from the tree.

The evening before our departure, the phone rang during dinner. Cheryl answered the phone and turned pale. She spoke for a little while, and then called me. I walked over to her and she said, "Marion is on the phone and she wants to talk to you. Take it in the den." I went into the den and closed the door. I picked up the phone and in a shaking voice, I said, "Hello."

I heard Marion's sweet voice and I started to cry. She was sobbing too. "Aaron," she said, "I love you. I always will, and I promise that I'll visit you the first chance I get. I need to get out of Boise. You didn't realize it then, but you were the lucky one. I have to hang up now. Please forgive me." I heard the click of the phone.

It was an all too brief, but enlightening conversation. I had regained two sisters I had believed were dead to me. I fell to my knees and thanked God before I returned to the dining room.

The time passed all too quickly, and it was time to leave. Adam told us that business brought him to San Francisco from time to time and he promised to call us when it happened, so that we could get together. Cheryl promised to call at least twice a week and made us promise to do the same. She also told me that Brad's suggestion of sending my folks a Christmas card would not work. She had been doing that every year without any response. Cheryl had finally conceded to herself that a relationship with her parents would never be. "If only Adam's parents were here," she would lament over and over. I decided to send a card anyway and sign it from Aaron and Bradley. That should zing them.

On the plane going home, Ben sat between us. At first we made small talk and then Ben confided in us. "I've whacked off with a friend a lot," he whispered, "but we never touched each other and I am still a virgin."

"I can tell you that that's a hell of a thing to be at your age," I said. "I was a virgin until I was eighteen," I added. "Don't worry your time will come."

Our dads were at the airport to pick us up, as usual. What would we do without them? Sam and Chris were in the house when we arrived from the airport. They took one look at the handsome youth, and Sam exclaimed, "Ben baby, you are drop dead gorgeous. This is going to be so easy."

Back home we were presented with a slight dilemma. Sam and Chris had taken over the guest room, and our third bedroom was furnished as an office. Where were we to house Ben? Once again our dads came to the rescue. They told Sam and Chris to use their guest room during Ben's stay. The two of them were moving into their dorm room the day after Labor Day anyhow. Then all of us would be empty nesters.

We couldn't really show Ben much of San Francisco because of work commitments. Fortunately Brad and I had bought Sam and Chris a used car for them to use to get back and forth from college so they had wheels, and they volunteered to show Ben the town. There would be a Youth Group meeting Friday night prior to services on Sunday and the three of them attended.

Luis Lopez was the young man our brothers wanted Ben to meet. He was one hundred percent Latino. His dark brown eyes were so seductive they could melt the coldest heart. His jet black hair was untamed and was all over his beautiful face. He had a Roman nose and a square chin. He stood only about 5'8" and was a good three inches shorter than Ben. His best attribute was that he always wore very tight jeans which accentuated his ample package.

Sam introduced the boys before the meeting. When they shook hands, their eyes fixed on each other. Sam smiled to himself. Luis and Ben sat together and when the meeting began, it was Luis who introduced Ben as a visitor from LA. During the meeting Sam and Chris noticed that Luis took Ben's hand and they smiled at each other.

When the meeting ended and the group was enjoying refreshments, Ben asked Sam and Chris if he thought Brad and I would mind if Luis slept over and spent the next day with them. They called us and we said it would be all right if it was OK with Luis's parents.

Sam drove Luis home so he could pack a bag. It was obvious that he was planning on more than a one night stand. While he was packing, Chris asked Mr. Lopez (Mrs. Lopez had died when Luis was a baby) if it would be all right if Luis spent some time at his brother's house where Ben was staying.

"You can keep that fucking faggot forever if you want. It would be OK with me if I never had to see his ugly puss again," Mr. Lopez spat out, and took another swig of his beer. When they got back in the car, Chris whispered to Sam, "I have a gut feeling that when Brad and Aaron see this boy and hear what happened, that he isn't going anywhere."

It was quite late when Sam and Chris delivered the boys. Ben introduced Luis and asked permission for him to bunk with him that night. Did we have a choice? Ben took Luis up to the guest room and Sam filled us in.

"Can you put him up for awhile? His dad sure doesn't want him to come back home." Chris said.   After the boys were settled in, they joined us downstairs. I made hot chocolate and cookies. My eyes were constantly on the two handsome young lads. Ben's face was even more beautiful in his joy. He was surrounded by people he didn't have to hide from. He was at peace. He was at home, and I think he was in love for the first time.

Luis was beaming too. His home life was hell, and now he was relaxed and happy. His eyes never left off looking at Ben. I knew the look of love when I saw it. Suddenly I adopted Luis just as Larry had adopted me so long ago.

Finally Sam and Chris went over to our dads' home and the boys scooted off to bed. We cleaned the dishes, shut the kitchen light, and ran to our bedroom.

The next morning, Sam and Chris came over to hang with the boys just as Brad and I were headed for some super market shopping. "Chuck and Larry are gone already," Sam announced. We left the four youngsters to enjoy the day.

Sam and Chris loaded the boys into their functional jalopy and took them for a tour of San Francisco, which included Muir Woods, Fisherman's Wharf, and Alcatraz Island. They spent the entire day touring and ate both lunch and dinner out. Strange as it seems, Luis had never visited these places.

"Too bad you kids are under age," Chris said. "We could take you to some of the gay bars." Chris and Ben were acting like big shots. They had just turned eighteen themselves a few months ago, and had not yet gone to a gay bar.

The next day, as we were getting ready to go to church, Brad told Ben that if he was uncomfortable and preferred not to go, it would be alright if he stayed at home.

"No way," Ben said, "All my new friends will be there, and you said we were all going to brunch after the service."

Ben, Luis, Sam and Chris all sat with the youth group at the back of the church, but at the social hour, Ben and Luis monopolized Reverend Clint. I don't know what they were talking about, but when they were finished all three participated in a group hug.

As the days drew nearer to Ben's departure and to Sam and Chris going off to college, there was a definite change in the two young boys. Sadness overtook them, and I caught them crying when they thought nobody was watching.

Finally Luis took the bull by the horns and called his father to tell him he was coming home.

"Don't bother, faggot," his father told him. "I already rented out your room."

Luis wasn't sure if he should cry or be joyous. When I told him that he was welcome to live with us, he decided to cry, but he cried tears of joy. Ben swore he would apply to college in San Francisco and told Luis that until then he would visit on every school holiday.

"I can go to college anywhere," Ben told Luis. "My parents left a trust fund for my college education."

"You'll be educated," Luis said. "You'll be ashamed of me."

"I could never be ashamed of you," Ben assured him.

"Who said you won't be educated?" I asked Luis. "I assure you that I'll see to your education, son." When I said 'son' Luis broke out crying and fell into my arms.

- CHAPTER EIGHTEEN -

Pickler and Underwood had an attorney on retainer. Luis's father was more than glad to relinquish his parental rights, especially when we offered him $5000.00 not to object. The attorney had no problem gaining us guardianship of Luis.

I transferred him to my school, and he lived with us until he left for college. Even then, our home was always his home. He even called Larry and Chuck, 'Grandpa.' I wanted him to be able to reach his father if he wanted to, but I didn't want Mr. Lopez to know exactly where he was living. I didn't trust the man. We bought Luis a cell phone when he first came to live with us, and he called his father to give him the number.

"I told you not to bother me," he yelled at Luis. "There's no way a faggot like you could be my son. Your mother cheated on me for sure, the cunt." Luis hung up shaking and sobbing, and never called his father again. He declared that if he was dead to his father, his father was dead to him.

We invited Cheryl and her family, Ben included, to spend the Thanksgiving and Christmas holidays with us. They accepted both invitations. We gave Cheryl, Adam and baby Aaron our bedroom. They told us that they had a portable crib for the baby. Ben and Luis used the guest room. Our dads had a three bedroom home so Sam and Chris used their guest room. The third bedroom was set up as a small den but it had a sleep sofa in it and Brad and I stayed there. The arrangements were more than satisfactory and enabled the whole family to be close by.

Adam decided that it was more convenient to drive up to San Francisco than to fly with a baby. They started out early Wednesday morning and arrived before dinner. Larry and Chuck invited us all to dinner that night and we had a festive pre holiday dinner. Our dads made a huge fuss over baby Aaron, and naturally they were prepared with plenty of baby gifts.

Thanksgiving was to be at our house. Brad's parents, the Hansons, Russ and Clint were invited also. It was too big a crowd for us to handle and we had it catered. The caterer was one of Russ's clients. He made sure that everything was perfect. He jokingly told us that he was reducing the price by twenty percent because the four teenagers offered such tasty eye candy.

Cheryl, Brad's mother and Sarah Hanson all had instant chemistry and they set about helping the caterers. Mostly they discussed the miracle of finding family members they thought were lost to them forever and the special joy of this Thanksgiving. Everyone played with baby Aaron. I prayed he wouldn't get sick. The teen agers tossed a football around in the back yard and as far as I was concerned they were four brothers united for the holiday.

Adam, bless him, told Luis that he was welcome to come and visit on any school holiday. The invitation was open and standing. Luis and Ben hugged Adam who had to cry for mercy, they were hugging him so hard. When Luis told Adam that he was interested in studying law, Adam invited him to LA for the summer to work in his office and do whatever odd jobs were needed. Luis nearly exploded with joy, and he and Ben could not stop hugging each other. What they were unaware of was that Adam would be paying Luis's meager salary from his own pocket. My parents had no clue that my sister had married such a fine human being, and even if they did, they wouldn't care. He wasn't a Mormon.

On Friday and Saturday a procession of friends and neighbors visited us, and my family fell in love with all of them. From the beginning, Cheryl and Adam were calling Larry and Chuck, Dad and Pop. Not unlike Brad and me when we first met Larry and Chuck, they needed the love of parents as much as we did. All of us who were at the Thanksgiving Day feast had more to be thankful for than on any other Thanksgiving Day I could remember.

Adam gathered up his family early Sunday morning after Thanksgiving, and started his long trek home. Nobody's eyes were dry including Dad and Pop. I'll bet that when they adopted me, they had no idea how large a family they were getting. I certainly didn't know. Be that as it may, they loved it!

Sam and Chris returned to school. Luis regained sole proprietorship of his bedroom and we regained ours. That Sunday night Brad and I made up for our forbearance of sex all holiday weekend.

After securing the house and turning off all the lights, Brad and I hurried to our bedroom. Luis's door was shut, but I listened to make sure he was in bed and maybe sleeping. We went into our room and shut the door. Then it was off to the shower to prepare our bodies for the pleasures to come. I guess we were hornier than I thought. Before we left the shower and fell exhausted into our bed, each of us had come once in the other's mouth and once in the other's ass. When we were finished making love, we stood in the shower wrapped in each other's arms, our tongues caressing. Our now limp cocks rubbed together as the water cascaded down our bodies, cleansing us.

Neither of us wanted it to end, but finally Brad shut the taps and we got out of the shower. We helped each other dry off and went to bed. We covered ourselves with the cool sheets and fell asleep locked in a mutual embrace. As I was falling asleep, it occurred to me that I loved Brad more each day.

Happily, a few doors down the street, our dads were enjoying a similar experience. Tonight was the first time in days that they had their house all to themselves. They too started in the shower intending only to wash each other, but like us, they ended up sucking and fucking each other. It was sheer torture for them to shut off the water, dry off, and go to sleep.

In time, we and our dads were done with love making for the moment, and we all fell into a profound and peaceful sleep.

Early the next morning, hours before dawn, while I was still in a twilight sleep, I heard a phone ringing somewhere off at a great distance. It took a few rings to realize that it was my phone. I willed myself awake and grabbed for the handset.

"Aaron, darling, I'm sorry to have awakened you," I heard Marion say. Before I could ask, she knew my thoughts. "Relax," she said, "Everything is fine. I'm here in San Francisco at the bus terminal. It's a long story, but the short version is that I ran away from home. I would have gone to Cheryl in LA, but I only had enough money to get to San Francisco. Can you come and get me, please." Then she started to cry.

"I'll be right there," I said.

By now Brad was fully awake and the two of us threw on a pair of shorts, tee shirts, and sandals. We didn't even bother with underwear. As we started to leave the room, there was Luis standing in the doorway in his birthday suit. "Not bad," I thought.

"What's going on?" he asked. We told him what we knew and Brad told him to go back to sleep.

"No way," he said. "I'll have coffee and bagels ready when you get back."

Brad drove into the nearly deserted terminal. I didn't see anyone, but then no young girl would wait outside alone. I jumped out of the car and ran into the terminal. I spotted her sitting alone on a bench in the corner. She had become the beautiful woman that the child had promised to be. "Marion," I yelled.

She looked up and spotted me. She bounded over to me and threw her arms around me. After some hugging and kissing, she said, "You've become a very handsome man, Aaron Jackson."

"And you are one red hot, foxy lady yourself, Marion Jackson," I returned the compliment. "Where's your luggage?" I asked.

"What you see, is what you get," she sobbed. I ran out with only my purse."

"Wow," I said. "Brad is out front in the car. You can tell us all about it on the way home."

We found Brad out front and I helped Marion into the back seat. I introduced her to Brad, but Marion's Mormon upbringing won out. She hesitated and finally decided not to shake Brad's homosexual hand. Hopefully he understood and ignored the slight.

Marion began: "I came home for Thanksgiving. There was just the three of us for dinner, but after dinner we got a visitor. A middle age, fat, sloppy looking, and very bald man came in, and we were introduced. Dad introduced him as my intended. He said that I didn't have to go back to school. The wedding was all set and planned for the first weekend in January. I panicked, but I politely waited for the gentleman to leave. I don't even remember his name.

Once he was gone, I erupted. I screamed that I would kill myself before I'd marry that monster. Dad slapped my face. Mom called me an ingrate. I grabbed my purse and ran out of the house. A few blocks away, I used my cell phone to call for a cab to take me to the Greyhound Terminal, and here I am."

"You're finally out of jail," I said. "Don't worry little sister. I've got plenty of money and I'll see to it that you finish your education. You have a home here with us. Cheryl took in her orphaned brother-in-law. Now it's our turn. We want you to have a home with us. Don't we Brad?"

"Marion," Brad said very softly, "Our home is your home for as long as you wish, but first you have to accept my relationship with your brother. We aren't monsters or sinners. We love each other. It's that simple. We don't have to make any excuses for being in love."

"I know that," Marion said, "but old habits and older beliefs are hard to break. I'm sorry." She reached forward and put her hand on Brad's shoulder. He reached up and put his hand on hers. The ice, as they say, was broken.

"Marion," I asked. Do you want to go back to BYU or would you like to transfer here?"

"Even though I've lost this semester, I'd rather transfer. I don't want THEM to know where I am. Cheryl has enough with a new baby and Adam's brother. I'm afraid you're stuck with me."

"You think so?" I asked. "Wait until you meet our family. I think you might be the one who's stuck. We'll try to enroll you in UCSF for the spring semester. You can live on campus. Brad's brother Sam just started his freshman year there and he lives on campus. We'll work on your transfer right away," I told her.

"As a footnote, little sister, Cheryl and her family are coming for Christmas. Our whole family, at least those of us who matter, will all be together for the holiday. Have you any clue how happy that makes me?"

"I promise, Aaron, I'll pay you back every cent. You shouldn't have to assume Dad's responsibilities."

"I know that I don't have to, but I sure want to. I assure you. It's not a financial burden for me. You have already paid me back by just being here with me."

"We have one minor problem," Brad reminded me.

"No," I said. "We'll put a sleep sofa in the den for Luis until Marion moves to the dorms. In the meantime he can use a sleeping bag I have in the hall closet."

"Who is Luis?" Marion asked. "How many people live with you?"

"Sometimes I think we run a motel, but right now it's just Luis. His father kicked him out just like I was kicked out and for the same reason. It was natural for us to take him in and assume guardianship over him. Besides he has a relationship with Adam's brother, Ben. It's a long story"

"It's getting too complicated for me. Give me time to absorb it all. In the meantime, I need to buy some basic clothes and toiletries, and I want to call Cheryl in the morning."

"Aaron has to teach his classes tomorrow, but I'll rearrange my appointments and take you shopping tomorrow morning, if it's OK with you," Brad said.

"Thank you," Marion said with a sob in her voice. "I also want to look for a job."

Brad remembered the promise Adam had made to Luis, and the fact that he would pay Luis's salary. He decided to extend the same offer to Marion.

"Look," he said, "it's only for a few weeks until the spring semester begins. We can always use some extra clerical help in my office. Does that sound like something you'd like to do?"

"Well, yes," Marion answered, "but what kind of office is it?"

"It's a CPA office," Brad told her. "Very conservative, no vice going on."

It took Marion a moment to realize that Brad was kidding, and when she did, she started to laugh. It was the first laughter I heard from her.

When we came into the house, dawn was just breaking. We were greeted by the odor of fresh brewed coffee. The kitchen table was set for four. The bagels, butter, jam, sugar and milk were all set out. Luis had remembered to dress. He was wearing short shorts and a ripped tee shirt and obviously nothing else. Man, that boy was hot.

When Marion was introduced to Luis, she shook his hand without cringing. We were all hungry and dug into the food that Luis had graciously prepared.

Suddenly Luis gasped, "Look at the time," he said looking over at me "We better get ready for school."

Within a couple of days, the sleep sofa was set up in the office and Luis's belongings were moved to the office closet. Marion was outfitted and temporarily occupied the guest room. She and Brad went up to UCSF and explained her situation. The school helped arrange for her high school and college records to be transferred and pending the transfer, she was accepted into her lower junior year. They also assigned her a room with a girl whose original room mate had dropped out of school. The room was in the same dorm as Sam and Chris. They went over to the dorm hoping to meet her. She was in the room and when the girls were introduced they liked each other immediately. Wendy asked Marion if she would like to join her and some friends Saturday evening and Marion accepted. Brad told Wendy he would drive Marion to the campus at the appointed hour, and Wendy said she would drive her home because Marion said she wanted to go to church with us on Sunday.

Then we went over to Sam and Chris's room. The door was closed and Brad knocked.

"Who is it?" Sam asked.

"It's your brother meathead," Brad answered.

The door opened immediately and there stood Chris and Sam naked. When they saw a girl with Brad, they both quick grabbed their gym shorts and put them on. "Sorry," Chris murmured.

"Living with all theses guys is going to be a challenge," Marion thought. "I'd better get used to it."

All day Saturday, Luis and our brothers helped Brad and me, and our dads, decorate our houses for Christmas. They also helped their parents. Marion worked alongside them and this activity took her mind off things. She took a break Saturday evening to meet Wendy, and she reported that her Saturday night out with her new girlfriends was a 'real blast.' "Wendy told everyone what a hunk you are, Brad, and they can't wait to meet you. Too bad they don't stand a chance," she said, laughing loudly.

On Sunday Marion had a chance to get to know our family. She, Sam and Chris bonded, just talking about what awaited her at UCSF. I think they whetted her appetite to get back to a school she could consider normal.

Our dads immediately added her to their list of adoptees. She met the Wilkinsons, the Hansons, Russ and Clint, our neighbors and Luis's entire youth group. It was Luis who introduced her as his sister. She was overwhelmed when I told her that I considered all of them to be family. "Every one of them loves me more than Mom and Dad ever loved me, or at least, they show me more love than Mom and Dad ever did."

On Monday morning, Brad took her to the office to begin her temporary position. Before getting started he introduced her to the staff. She already knew Russ, but Jamie and Jim were all over her with hugs and kisses.

"More family," Brad explained. After all the introductions were made, Brad asked, "Where's Craig?" He was referring to Craig Billings, the only straight male in the firm.

"He's at a client," Jim said, "but he should be back before lunch. Brad turned Marion over to the office manager, and she got her started on some menial office chores, which Marion was more than happy to be doing.

Before the morning was an hour old, one of the girls in the office asked Marion to have lunch with her and Marion accepted. At about 11:30 AM a young man came into the office. The receptionist said, "Good morning Craig." Marion looked up and her heart stopped. The young man looked like the man of her dreams, her fantasy lover. She had no way of knowing it at the time, never having met him, but Craig bore a strong resemblance to her brother-in-law Adam. They were similar in height and build and they could have been first cousins. They both had blue eyes, but Craig had blond hair. Adam's hair was the color of chestnut. It was all Marion could do not to stare at him.

At first Craig did not notice Marion, but the office manager said, "Let me introduce you to Marion Jackson. She'll be working with us for a few weeks. She's Brad's sister in law." When Craig shook Marion's hand, he thought he might faint. He couldn't breathe. He literally willed himself to draw a breath. Standing before him was the most beautiful girl he had ever laid eyes on.

"Please, God," he prayed silently, "don't let her be a lesbian. This is the girl I want to marry." He muttered something about welcome aboard and rushed into Brad's office. He closed the door behind him. He tried to speak but he was still hyperventilating.

"What?" Brad asked.

"Will you kill me if I ask Marion out on a date? I swear I'll be the perfect gentleman."

Brad started to laugh. "She's over eighteen," he said. Just pray she doesn't reject you."

"How did you feel when you first laid eyes on Aaron?" Craig asked.

Brad thought for a second and said, "You'd better ask her out quick before someone else does."

"I'm safe in *this* office until she goes out to lunch," Craig joked.

"I think she's having lunch with Margie," Brad said.

"They don't know it yet, but Margie and Marion are having lunch with me."

As Craig turned to leave the office, Brad noticed a bulge in Craig's crotch area. He had never noticed that before or maybe he hadn't looked.

- Chapter Nineteen -

Craig was pretty near useless in the office all week. He kept gawking at Marion. I hate to say it, but Brad told me that he was drooling like a dog in heat. He had lunch with her every day, but there were always other people with them. He asked her out on a date Saturday evening, and she said she would let him know.

"What should I do about Craig?" she asked me and Brad that evening. "I'm crazy about him, but I don't want him to know just yet. I want to play hard to get."

"Let's find out what he's made of," I said. "Tell him you don't want to go out on a date Saturday evening, but you would like to get to know him better. Invite him to dinner instead, and I have a great idea."

When we were alone in bed that night, Brad asked, "What have you got up your sleeve?"

"You'll see," I said. "After Saturday night, he'll either run a country mile or he'll be one of the family."

"Just don't do anything you'll regret," Brad warned me. "Marion is crazy about this guy and he has just about stopped functioning for love of her."

"If that's true we have nothing to worry about," I stated emphatically.

I made sure that Luis, Sam, and Chris would be home on Saturday night to have dinner with us and meet Marion's "boy friend." I also invited our dads. Usually all of us refrain from showing affection to each other when straight people are around, but I instructed each couple to be extra affectionate in Craig's company. "Kiss a lot and hold hands. Act like the lovers you are. If he's going to be uncomfortable, then it's too bad about him. If he loves Marion as much as he says, it won't bother him one bit."

"You're playing with fire," Brad warned me. "Marion might not like the game. Craig already works with predominantly gay people and many of our clients are gay so I don't know what you are trying to prove."

"That's different," I said. "That's his work place. This is the queer family he seems to want to marry into."

Brad just shook his head sadly. "I don't see why we can't just be us," he said and sulked away.

On Saturday evening, I made sure everyone was in the house before Craig arrived. My dads were over early anyway. They and Marion helped me prepare the dinner. Brad was on strike, thoroughly opposed to what I was about to do. I had met Craig a couple of times so I made sure I answered the door when he arrived. The dear boy had two bouquets of flowers with him.

He thrust one at me and said, "This is for your table, Aaron. I really appreciate your invitation." Marion had come up behind me. He handed her the other bouquet and said, "These are for the most beautiful woman in the world." That was sweet, but I wanted to puke. This dude was way over the love sick hill.

I took his arm and steered him into the living room. First I'd like you to meet Marion's dads, and ours," I added. I introduced him to Chuck and Larry, and reminded him that Chuck was the company banker.

"It's a pleasure," he said as he stuck out his hand. My dads would have none of that. We had rehearsed the whole thing. They grabbed Craig and hugged him tightly while kissing him on the cheek. I couldn't tell if Craig was embarrassed or not, but he smiled cordially at them.

Then I introduced him to Marion's 'kid brother,' Luis, who grabbed him in a bear hug and kissed him on the lips. Craig's reaction was minimal. Marion was the one with her mouth open.

"I'd introduce you to her other two brothers Sam and Chris, but they seem to be occupied." Sam and Chris were sitting on the sofa making out like crazy. They may have been acting, but I was afraid they were going a little too far. They might not be able to stand up if they were introduced.

All through the evening the couples were smooching in front of Craig. When I tried to kiss Brad, he rebuffed me. He was having none of this game. Craig seemed perfectly comfortable with it. Was he acting? Did Brad give him a head's up in the office?

At one point during the dinner, someone casually mentioned that Chuck was a professor at Berkeley and taught English Literature. Craig's eyes lit up. "My dad teaches Philosophy there. Maybe you know him? Max Billings."

"Oh my God," Chuck screamed out. "I never made the connection. Of course, you're Max's boy. I met you when you were a baby and your folks had just adopted you. I don't know why we haven't been around since. I guess everybody is too busy.

Suddenly Chuck burst out laughing. "Aaron, the joke's on you. Craig has two dads. He was raised by a gay couple. The question is, how does this affect Marion's feelings for Craig? I wonder if his parents can accept the fact that their little boy is straight." That thought must have struck Chuck as a very funny twist because he burst out laughing.

"Aaron," Marion blurted out. "What have you been up to?" She jumped up from the table and asked Craig to please come with her. She took him into the den and closed the door.

"Does that mean I can act normal?" Luis asked.

"I don't know. I was enjoying myself," Sam said, grabbing for Chris's crotch.

Everyone grew silent waiting for Marion and Craig to come out of the den. When I could stand it no longer, I knocked on the door. "Please come out," I begged. "Craig I need to apologize." The silence continued so I started to open the door. Marion and Craig were locked in each other's arms, hugging tightly, kissing longingly. I closed the door.

"I think it will be all right," I said.

Later when everything returned to normal and we were all having dessert, and laughing at each other, Brad asked Craig, "How come you never told anyone at the office that your dads are gay?"

"I wanted to be hired on my merits, not on my gay background so to speak. But if I hadn't been surrounded by gay guys all my life, I probably would never have applied at Pickler and Underwood. I just knew I'd be more comfortable in a gay environment. For sure I knew I wouldn't hear any homophobic jokes like I had to put up with all through school. I was picked on just as much as the gay guys were. If only those idiots knew what great parents I have."

"I am a class A jerk," I said. "I have a talent for self destruction, don't I Brad?"

Brad could only nod in agreement.

Just then the phone rang. I went to answer it. It was Clint on the other end. I listened intently to him and turned pale. After I hung up everybody looked at me. It was obvious that something had happened.

"Speaking of self destruction," I said, "Carl Gilmore is dead. He got into some kind of fight at the prison and he was knifed to death. The warden told Clint that there were dozens of inmates with motive. He asked Clint to drive up to the prison and identify the body. He's going to turn the body over to Clint for disposition. Clint said he will let us know when he makes plans for the funeral."

I knew how Brad must be feeling, but how did I feel? I had long been rid of Carl, but I felt a sense of closure and I was at peace with it. Carl made his bed and he smothered himself in it.

The mood remained sober for a bit longer and then things began to lighten up. Brad kissed me at last and asked if I was all right. I nodded yes. Luis, Sam, Chris, Marion and Craig went into the living room and engaged in some kind of family bonding ritual. Mostly the talk was about school. "When do we meet your folks?" I heard Chris ask Craig as Brad, my dads and I began to clean up the mess left behind.

The next Monday at Pickler and Underwood, Craig let everyone know that he had two dads. He wanted to be the one to let everyone know before they heard it from someone else. The attitude around the office was, "So?"

At Berkeley, Chuck sought out Craig's dad. Occasionally they ran into each other and said a few words, but things were different now. Max's adopted son was about to become engaged to his adopted daughter. Chuck caught up to him just as he was completing a class. The two men embraced warmly.

"When Craig told me what happened last Saturday night, Nate and I were speechless for an hour. It's a tiny world after all. We can't wait to meet Marion. When the kids make it official we want to make a family party at our place," Max announced.

"That's fine," Chuck said, "but we shouldn't have to wait that long to get together. Let's you and Nate, Larry and I have dinner at Alfredo's Friday night. They're clients of Brad's and we get a discount there. It doesn't hurt that the food there is so good."

They made arrangements and parted with another hug.

The Christmas dinner guest list was growing by leaps and bounds. Marion, Craig and Craig's dads were additions to what had been the Thanksgiving Day list. Even Brad, the accountant, wasn't sure just how many we were having. Near as we could figure out we would be seventeen adults and a baby. We definitely decided to have everything catered. Once again we engaged Russ's clients, and not a moment too soon. They were catering several parties on Christmas Day and they could only handle one more. We got in under the wire.

Sleeping arrangements were no problem. Brad and I stayed with Brad's parents. Sam and Chris stayed with Chris's parents. Luis and Ben stayed at our dads. Cheryl, Adam, Marion and the baby stayed in our house. Hey, what are families for? I couldn't help wondering what my parents in Boise were thinking as they celebrated the holiday with no children and no grandchild. I wondered if they even knew of baby Aaron's existence. Well it was totally their loss.

Gifts! Now there was a problem. Brad and I spent the weekend before Christmas buying and wrapping gifts. It was difficult, but in the end we thought we had gotten the perfect gift for everyone. We also spent an hour or two going through the house and making the decorations and other items child proof since baby Aaron had begun to crawl. We tried to think of everything, but only time would tell if we succeeded.

The last thing I did before everyone was due to arrive was to send a Christmas card to my parents. I must have been bitten by the Ghost of Christmas Future because I softened everything I had intended to tell them. Instead I enclosed a picture of Brad and me, a picture of Cheryl's family that I had taken at Thanksgiving, and finally a picture of Marion and Craig which I took for the occasion. I also enclosed a card with my address and telephone number. I wrote:

Dear Mom and Dad:

I am living in San Francisco where I teach high school math. I share my life with Bradley Wilkinson. He's a partner in a successful CPA firm. You will be pleased to know that we attend church every single Sunday, and the pastor is a personal friend of ours.

Recently I found Cheryl, and Brad and I visited her in Los Angeles. Her husband, Adam, is a lawyer and one of humanity's true gentlemen. Their baby is named Aaron (after Adam's father) and Adam's orphaned teen age brother lives with them.

Marion is living with me and will resume her college education when the spring semester begins. She recently got engaged to be engaged to one of Brad's co-workers, Craig Billings. Craig isn't a CPA yet, but it's in his future.

I am enclosing pictures of all of us. Should you ever wish to contact me, your call would always be welcome. In spite of everything, your children still love you. God bless you and a Merry Christmas to both of you.

Love,

Your son, Aaron

It was the happiest Christmas that I had ever spent. Brad and I were surrounded with love. Everyone I cared about in the world was with me. They all shared Christmas morning with me at my church, no matter what religious beliefs they held.

I didn't hear from my parents immediately, but just after the New Year I received a note from them.

Aaron, we could never look you in the face. You and your Bradley are an abomination in the eyes of God. Your sisters are no better. They have disrespected us and married outside of our church. There is no greater sin than to disrespect a parent. Until all of you are ready to repent and apologize, do not contact us again.

It was what I expected. I sent a copy of the letter to Cheryl and showed it to Marion. She and I had a good cry, but then I said to her, "It's really funny, Marion, I'm not at all sad. Now I can forget about them and put them behind me. You've seen how loving my real family is. They're your family now too, and Craig's. I'm finally at peace. I hope with Craig you can find the same serenity that I have found with Brad."

Brad had been standing in the doorway, and heard what I said to Marion. "I love you too," he said. He put his arms around me and kissed me. With Brad's help I was finally at peace with the world, and with God.

- About the Author -

Hank Brooks was born in Brooklyn, NY and lived most of his adult life in and around the New York City area.

He is very active in SAGE, a senior advocacy group for gay men and women.

He has three children and five grandsons. He is a retired CPA, and now lives with his partner, Leo, in Coconut Creek, Florida.

Hank Brooks is also the author of ***An Anthology of Erotica - Gay Love Stories, Fathers*** and ***Sons, A Family Affair*** and ***Impossible Love.*** Available at Amazon.com, TheNazcaPlainsCorp.com or your local bookstore.

FATHERS
and SONS

a novel by HANK BROOKS

A BONER
BOOK

AN ANTHOLOGY OF EROTICA
Gay Love Stories

by HANK BROOKS

Impossible Love

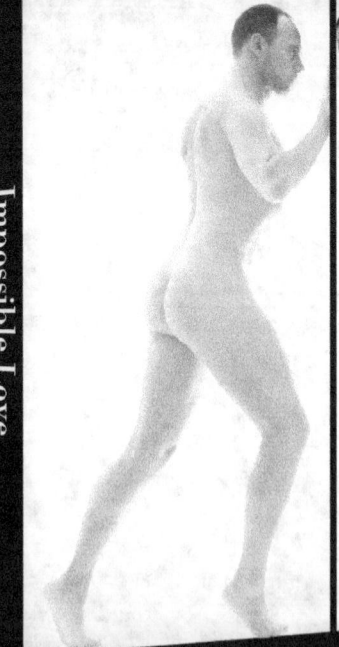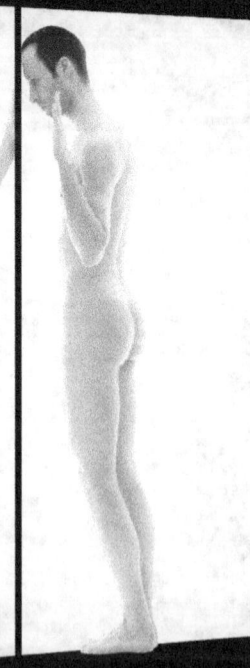

a novel by

Hank Brooks

A
Boner
Book

A
Boner
Book

BROOKS

A FAMILY AFFAIR

A Family Affair

and Other Erotic Gay Tales by

Hank Brooks